# Touching Other Lives

## Volume 1
## Episodes 1 - 7

### by

# Margaret Gregory

TRIED & TRUSTED INDIE PUBLISHING

# Touching Other Lives

## Volume 1
### Episode List

# Episode 1

## The Wrong Kind of Friend?
### (Annie's POV)

### <u>Chapter 1</u>

I felt my feet slowing as a familiar reluctance set in. I stopped, adjusted my backpack and reached into my blazer pocket.

As soon as my hand touched Dad's handkerchief, my mind seemed drawn to another place. Not the neighbourhood street, but a board room. Yesterday, was Dad's first day as project leader for a new housing development. Today was my first day at yet another school. Touching these memories of his first day – when he had soon had everyone happy to work with him – I wished I had inherited his way with people.

The memory played out and I forced myself to begin walking again and swapped the hanky for the hand drawn map my mother had given me of the route to school. I needed to go left at the next road. She would have driven me to school today, and been a bit late for her new job, but I wasn't ready to jump right into things. The walk let me prepare my mind. If I had ever learnt anything from constantly switching schools, it was that I had to make friends, not wait for others to befriend me.

Up ahead, a figure in a similar coloured blazer had stopped and seemed to be doing up a shoelace. Idly, I wondered if he too was reluctant to face the start of another year. He was still fiddling with his shoe when two cyclists rode by – each with the same colour blazer, the same type of bag as my second hand one. They called out something to the figure ahead, but I didn't catch it.

I caught up to the boy as he hitched his bag onto his shoulders. "Hello," I said, and he spun around, his face flushed.

"Who are you?" He moved away, as if expecting me to attack him.

"Annie Jamieson. Who are you?"

He paused before admitting, "Martin. What do you want?"

"Well, I'm on my way to school. I have a map, but I wasn't sure I was still on the right route." A bit of a lie, but hey, a chance to make a friend. "Would you mind if I walked with you?"

"Ah, no...I guess."

"What class will you be in?" He looked about my age.

"Year 10. You?"

"Same. Do you know which class? I was told there would be four."

"Not yet. We'll have an assembly first up. We will find out then."

"I have to go to the admin office first. I've got to give them my records from all my previous schools."

"Huh! How many have you been to?"

"Too many. Anyone that didn't know that my Dad moves around from project to project might think I kept getting kicked out."

"What's he do?"

"He's an architect."

"And your mum? Does she work?"

"She's a nurse. She works at the Royal Women's. What do your folks do?"

The silence warned me that was a touchy subject. "My Dad's unemployed right now. Usually he is a labourer, or a brickie."

"Do you have a mum?"

"Nope."

I figured that explained why Martin's clothes smelt like they hadn't been washed since the end of last year.

We had reached the road and turned. Five hundred metres ahead, three buses were at the kerb, and a long line of cars were waiting to turn into a driveway.

"The school's just up there," Martin offered. "You'd do better to go on ahead."

"I was hoping you could point me in the direction of the admin."

He sighed. "Okay."

I ignored the looks that seemed aimed at me. I was an unfamiliar face, wearing a slightly too large uniform that I had hitched up a bit, and a noticeably worn backpack.

I went to where Martin pointed, and he went towards the large building that was both assembly hall and indoor basketball courts. If I wasn't held up, I would just be able to get there on time.

On entering the auditorium, I saw people were grouped according to year level – indicated by big numbers on stands at the front. I hurried to where the year tens were and sidled up next to Martin who was standing at the back. He had removed his blazer. When I grinned at him, he stopped scowling to smile back briefly.

By the time I found my new homeroom, I had discovered that Martin was far from being the most popular guy around. The body odour he exuded probably had a lot to do with it. Was there something else? He had been polite enough to me, even if a bit nervy.

No one else had done more than look at me as I selected a locker on the lower level. Most of the class had shoved forward, trying for one of the upper ones. I put all my new stationery in the left side of the locker and my bag on the right. I was at the end, and Martin selected the locker next to mine.

"Can you hold this for a minute," Martin asked softly.

Seeing no reason not to, I took the blazer he had folded inside out. Immediately, my mind filled with an image. Martin being jostled by two taller boys, and him ending on the dusty ground.

That's all I got, as Martin took his blazer back. He had to nudge me.

"You alright?"

"Yeah!" I stood up and looked for an empty seat, as the teacher told us to be seated quickly.

Martin didn't follow me to my preferred position near the front. To see the board properly I had to be close, until my glasses were fixed. The girl who was seated nearest gave me a glance and, in spite of the injunction to "settle down and listen", whispered, "You'd be better off keeping away from Martin Kemple. They found drugs in his locker last year."

If that were the case, maybe I should. Getting a bad reputation on my first day wasn't a good idea. However, I didn't think he seemed like the type. The odd manifestation I had when I touched his blazer gave me the idea he was being bullied. Or did it mean something else? I really didn't know the guy.

Asking Martin was not going to happen. It would mean admitting what I knew, and how I knew and having to take the associated ridicule of being a 'freak'.

I had stopped thinking of this 'ability' as being my active imagination at work, as my Mum had proposed. It had once shown two of my friends coming out of the school canteen with wads of money wrapped in their hankies. They had been found out without me saying anything, but that time I had been happy to change schools again.

I had to go back to admin at the first break to pick up the records I had left for them to copy. As I passed the senior teachers office, I heard part of a tirade about someone's sloppy uniform. On my return, I saw Martin emerging from there. He glanced my way, a scowl back on his face, but stalked off without a greeting.

I stopped. *Should I say something?*

"Thank you, Miss Jamieson," the teacher said gravely. "We will look into the matter."

"Thanks." I didn't add his name. He hadn't told me who he was, probably assuming that I already knew.

"However, are you aware of the school's dress code?"

*Huh?* "No." I glanced down at my dress. It wasn't too short or anything.

"You were sent a letter with your school email log in and other details. That would have been two weeks ago."

"We left our old address about then, Sir. We only arrived here on the weekend. I expect the letter is at the post office."

"Well, we expect our students to wear their blazers all the time, except during sport or lab sessions. If it is very hot, we will make an announcement to remove them."

"Okay, thanks."

"And the young ladies should not be hitching up their dresses."

My face grew hot. "Oh, it's just that I didn't have time to take the hem up. You see our..."

His stern look silenced me. He wasn't going to take excuses. He took a pad from beside him on the desk and wrote something. "This is just a warning, but I expect you will have the problem solved by tomorrow. You need to give the slip to your homeroom teacher."

"Yes, Sir."

"You can go."


Once outside, I hitched my dress again so it hung evenly. The jumper I was wearing hid the extra four inches of fabric and the belt holding it up.

Trying to forget the unexpected reprimand, I headed for the library to get my textbooks. They were second hand ones too –

like my bag and uniform.

"Hey, new girl!"

I turned and saw some girls from my class, sitting on the bricked edge of a flower bed. Grinning, I told them, "I'm Annie Jamieson."

"How come you are coming here now?" one demanded.

"Because I am living down here now."

"So, where were you before?" The second speaker, like the first, didn't offer her name. She had dark brown hair, and the first had been a blond.

"Parramatta. In New South Wales."

"I didn't think they had room for new students this year." The first speaker eyed me. "Or are you one of the charity cases."

*Jerk! Charity case indeed.* "Sorry, I don't know your name yet."

"Gail." The name must have been surprised out of her. The others were Helen, Jackie and Claire.

"My dad is paying the same fees as yours are," I said, keeping my irritation in check.

"But you have all second hand stuff," Claire blurted.

"Ah that! We move around a lot, and since I probably won't be here next year, it's no use buying new stuff."

I grinned then, because all four faces betrayed their distaste at the thought. "Anyway, I need to get to the library. I'll catch you at lunch, okay?"

Gail waved me away. I doubted they would wait for me at the second break.


I was challenged by two seniors outside the library. "What are you doing in here during break?" the boy asked.

"I need to collect my text books."

The girl said, "They were meant to be collected last week."

"I only moved into our new place on Saturday! Anyway, it was arranged for me to get them today."

Having no comeback to that, the boy asked, "Why don't you have your blazer on?"

I sighed. "Because I didn't know I was meant to. I do now, since one of the teachers just told me and I can't get it until I can get back to my locker."

"Did he give you an orange slip?" the boy went on.

"Yeah, and it's not fair. Will I have to wait until the end of the break to put my books in my locker?"

"Ask the librarian for a passage pass," the girl told me.

As I pushed the library door open, I wondered if I needed a pass to use the girls loo's too.

The librarian was friendly, and I had a tour of the area on the way to where my books were waiting.

"There you are. All is paid for. Is there anything else I can do for you?"

"Can I get a passage pass so I can get these books back to my locker?"

"Certainly, Annie. Just come back to the desk."

By the time I had swapped my books for my blazer and visited the girls' facilities, the break was nearly over.

Maths, my favourite subject, was next. I discovered however, that I had been put in a basic maths class and not the advanced maths class. I tried to tell Mr Tucker when he was walking around checking our work, but he simply said to see him at the end of class.

On his second walk around he asked, "Finished already?"

I had. The work was too easy.

"Have you checked your answers?"

I looked at him. "Yes."

"Show me your working out."

"I did it in my head."

He frowned but was polite enough. "In this class, and in exams,

I expect to see the working out."

"I did this stuff last year."

Tucker, of course, had the last word. "Consider it revision."

The girl next to me, who'd said she was Naomi, murmured, "He's always like that."

I turned and gave her a grin. This school was nothing like the last three.

Later, when Tucker was occupied with another student, my neighbour murmured, "If you like, you can hang with us at lunch. We usually eat near the music prac rooms."

My answer was a smile and a nod.


By the time I had explained to Tucker that I was meant to be doing year 11 maths as part of the schools accelerator program, and that the school now had my previous records, everyone else had disappeared. I put my stuff away, got my lunch. Naomi was waiting outside for me.

Her friend welcomed me with a smile too, and I took the opportunity to ask about other pitfalls to avoid. When I spotted a familiar group nearby, I asked, "Who are those guys with Gail?" They were looking our way and I had a bad feeling that I knew who they were.

"Tom Logan, he's year twelve. She has a thing for him. Claire likes his brother, Gerry."

I tried to convince myself that they couldn't know that I had reported their bullying of Martin.


While getting out what I needed for the afternoon's English class, I was almost hit on the head by a pencil case.

"Sorry," came the voice from above as I passed it back up. I spotted a letter that must have fallen too, and when I picked it up, another of my odd day dreams began.

"... which one is she? ...The one at the end, brown hair in a pony tail..."

The letter was snatched from me by one of the girls and I shivered while closing my locker. As I stood, I had a whiff of Martin Kemple.

"Keep out of my business, Jamieson, okay?"

"But..."

"I don't know how you knew about the Logan's but I can handle them. I don't need your help and you don't need those two coming after you."

### Chapter 3

"Hey Jamieson!"

I recognized Martin's voice but kept walking. Someone ran up behind me.

"What do you want? I thought you didn't need me for anything."

"I didn't mean it that way," Martin said, coming up to walk beside me. "I meant help dealing with those Logan idiots. Do you want company on the way home?"

*Did I?* "I'll think about it."

"I know a short cut. It takes off half a block. It's the back way into the school."

"Alright."

"It's down past the tennis courts."

I could see the courts, and cars moving along some side street on the far side. "Do students get picked up down here?"

"No. Parents have to use the front drive. Some of the teachers come in this way though. Mostly it's deliveries and the rubbish truck. They don't stop us leaving this way on foot."

"And you don't need some permission slip?" I scowled, still annoyed by getting into trouble on my first day.

"Who gave you that warning slip? Old Gill?" Martin asked, abruptly.

"He didn't introduce himself. Probably assumed I knew who he was by divine inspiration. Like I was supposed to know the contents of a letter I haven't got yet. The office door said Allen."

"Allen's on leave until later in the year. Gill is acting Headmaster."

"Dark hair, balding on top?" I asked.

"Yup. Were you sent to him?"

"No, but I saw you being rolled in the dust and didn't want you in more trouble."

"So, you heard him going on, did you?"

"Just a bit. I was going to admin."

"Well...Thanks. You didn't have to and I doubt if anyone else would have."

"For what it was worth! He said he'd look into things and then told me off for not having my blazer on and for hitching up my dress. Implied I should have known, since the information was in that damn letter they sent. Wouldn't listen when I tried to say all our stuff only arrived on Sunday, and our mail is probably waiting for us at the nearest Post Office."

"He's a stickler for doing things by the book."

"Well it isn't fair! Anyway, why do you still not have your blazer on?"

"It's dirty and torn a bit."

"Did you get a warning too?"

"No, detention. Look, you really don't want to get on his bad side. He holds grudges."

"Nice man!"

"He must have spoken to them, because Tom wasn't happy when I met him at lunch."

"Why do you put up with them?"

"They were okay until their mum married into money. Now they think they're bigshots."

"Do they have money to throw around?"

"Their step father gives them an allowance, but it really isn't much."

"Must have Gail and those others fooled, since they hang around them. Do you reckon all the girls in their classes have them figured out?"

Martin laughed. "Probably. Uh oh, speak of the devil..."

Up ahead, near a group of several trees, two tall figures in the school's uniform were in a huddle with a slightly shorter and very scruffy looking figure. One of the boys looked up, and abruptly, the scruffy figure moved out of sight. Both boys were stuffing something into their pockets and one dropped a yellowish piece of paper.

We kept on the path, but the boys, with hands in pockets, strode towards us.

"Tell your girlfriend to mind her own business, cuz," the one I recognized as Tom Logan drawled.

"She's not my girlfriend!" Martin said, as I said, "I'm not his girlfriend."

Tom and his brother leered in disbelief. They moved even closer until they both sneezed.

"I don't like people who make trouble," Tom insisted.

Even though I knew, I demanded, "Who do you think you are to threaten us?" *I could act ignorant on my first day.* "I don't even know who the hell you are!"

"We're prefects." They introduced themselves, and accused, "You tried to set Pete Gill on us."

I let my brows rise as if this were a revelation. "So those two bullies that I saw were two far from perfect prefects?"

"Stop being smart, Jamieson," Gerry warned.

"I call it as I see it, Logan. At my last school, there was a zero tolerance towards bullying policy. I reported two boys, roughing up a shorter one. I had only been on the school grounds ten minutes, had never set eyes on either of you before – but thank you for the introduction. I'll look to both of you for my inspiration for best behavior."

A look of uncertainty passed between the two boys and they began to edge away.

"I could tell Gail and Clare what you are really like...." I decided to walk off and let them take that as a warning to leave me alone. Martin waited a bit, and then hissed some sharp words to them.

The paper they'd dropped had blown across to the path and I bent to pick it up. It was actually an envelope and still looked new.

The vision that hit me was so vivid and forceful that I nearly stumbled.

The man, the one who had been talking to the Logan brothers, was evil. His hand had a spider tattoo on it. There'd been drugs in that envelope, exchanged for money. I had a brief glimpse of the man's scarred face and long black greasy hair.

Once again Martin nudged me. "You off in a trance again?"

"I'm fine," I said, but I wasn't. My legs felt like jelly. "Martin, did you tell those two my name?"

"Gill might have."

"I didn't even know who they were when I spoke to him. He must have had a fair idea, then."

"Could be," Martin agreed without explaining.

"Why would he tell them my name?"

Martin shrugged. "Just keep away from them."

"People have been telling me to do the same to you."

"Up to you."

I wanted to growl, but kept silent until I had mentally counted to ten. "I can't see a reason to. You were nice to me this morning, you aren't being crude or trying to hit on me. If you weren't wearing that foul deodorant…"

"That's none of your business!"

"Sorry. I was commenting, not accusing. It makes me want to sneeze."

We had reached a small car park area, and beyond that was an open metal gate. "So, where does this lead?"

"Tennison Street. It comes off the main road."

I was trying to picture the map I'd had that morning, so when we reached the street, I shrugged off my backpack to look for it.

Martin asked, "What are you doing?" and then said something under his breath. "We need to get going."

He seemed to be jigging on the spot, and I sensed he was uneasy.

A car pulled up alongside us, and two people emerged. I was still checking my bag when they said, "We need you both to come with us."

I spun around and stood up. "Who are you?"

A hand drew out some ID, and the man said, "Police."

Martin was staring at the ground. *He'd known! But why? How?*

"They shouldn't keep you," Martin whispered as the two officers gestured us to the car. They took our bags and put them in the luggage compartment.

My mind was trying to picture what my folks would think if the police rang them. Then, as soon as I touched the seat inside, I wanted to be sick. Too many fleeting, overlapping images – impressions from countless people who had sat there before me – forced their way into my awareness. I forced my hand into my pocket to touch my Dad's hanky, and I found I could breathe again.

"What's going on?" I asked Martin.

"I don't know," he said, but I was sitting close to him and I was sure that he had more than a vague idea. I recalled Naomi, the girl in my class, saying, "They found drugs in my locker last year."

Then Martin was saying, "You have nothing to hide." *Did that mean that he did?*

For the ride from school to the police station, I didn't say anything. Their car radio was emitting cryptic remarks that explained nothing.

As we were escorted into the station, passersby stared. Our school uniforms were distinctive and I guessed the school would not be impressed if they heard. Martin and I were separated and I went into a small room with four chairs and a table. A female officer followed and asked, "What is your name?"

I told her, "Annie Jamieson."

"How old are you?"

"Fifteen."

"How can we get in touch with your parents?"

I wanted Mum or Dad with me right then. "You'll have to

text them. Dad has meetings all day and will probably be home late. I don't know when Mum's shift at the hospital will finish. She doesn't carry her phone around."

"Do you have their work numbers?"

"No."

"Which hospital does your Mum work at?"

"She just started today at the Royal Women's."

"Wait here. We will come back to see you."

"Hey! Why am I here anyway?"

"We think you can help us."

"Oh! I don't know how."

"Just wait here."

My watch told me that it was almost 4pm. Mum might even try ringing me, but my phone was in my bag – turned off. If she rang home, and I didn't answer, she'd worry.

The longer I waited, the worse I felt. It was nearly six when Mum was escorted into the room. I flew at her.

"Now can I find out what this is all about?" my Mum demanded.

"We need to ask your daughter some questions."

"Well, get on with it!" I insisted. "I've got homework to do and a dress to fix up before I get into trouble tomorrow."

"Sit down then," invited the woman, now accompanied by a male officer.

I'd been pacing the room, not wanting to touch the table in case it was like touching the seats in the police car. I put my chair right next to Mum's, so I was nearly touching her.

"How well do you know Martin Kemple?" The woman was taking the lead here.

"I met him on the way to school this morning."

The woman seemed to be waiting for me to say more.

"Well, I did! I just started at the school today. He was walking to school, so was I. It seemed like a chance to start making friends."

"You have changed schools quite regularly. Why is that?"
*Who had she been talking to? The Acting Head?*
I let my mother answer that.

"We move, depending on where my husband needs to be. He just finished overseeing the construction of a new shopping complex in Parramatta. Now he is project manager for a housing redevelopment in Dandenong."

"Tell me what you know about this envelope."

"You went through my stuff!"

That elicited no excuse, just silence for me to answer.

What I knew in the way they meant was minimal, what I knew otherwise...well, if I told them that they wouldn't believe it. Heck, my mother wouldn't either.

"That's an envelope that I picked up off the ground."

"Have a think. Where might this have come from?"

"On my way out of the back entrance of the school, it blew across from the right hand side, onto the path. It looked clean enough to re-use, so I picked it up."

"Are there rubbish bins over that way?"

"I don't know."

"Was there anyone else around, besides Martin Kemple?"

Huh! They've been talking to him...

"Well, there were other kids leaving that way. It's a short cut, Martin said. Tom and Gerry Logan were hanging around. They were talking to someone, then came over to lord it over us."

"Can you describe the person? Was it a student or a teacher?"

"I don't think it was either. No uniform, and too scruffy for a teacher."

"How good a look did you get?"

This was a tricky question, since my distance vision isn't that good. "Not really clear. The person had dark trousers, a khaki top, and dark hair to the shoulders."

"Anything else?"

*Should I?*

"Well, I only had a quick glance, but the person's face seemed distorted, and reddish, and there was something black on the back of one hand."

"How far away from this person were you?"

I estimated the distance and told her. My mother had to butt in. "How can you see that far? I still have to get your glasses fixed."

"I said it wasn't clear."

"You aren't just imagining things, Annie?" my mother asked, warningly.

"No!"

"You mentioned the Logan boys. When did you meet them?"

"About then."

"What did they want?"

"Probably to bully Martin some more. They told me to keep out of their business."

"You said you just met them," my inquisitor commented.

"They claim to be prefects..." I began, and went onto describe my day. I stated what I had seen in my mind as fact. They had roughed Martin up.

"What did Kemple say about that?"

"To mind my own business and he didn't need help dealing with them."

The woman asked some general questions about when we arrived in Bellfield and our movements, and then took some photos from a folder. "Do any of these people seem familiar?"

I looked along the line of six mugshots, came to the last and froze. "Him."

"How can you be so sure?" The woman was leaning towards me now.

*Hell! They will think me crazy but...*

I described what I had seen when I touched the envelope – but kept it to a feeling of 'bad', the image of the spider tattoo, and the sense that the envelope had contained drugs.

"Call it imagination, but I have never seen that bloke before."

The woman studied me awhile, then collected the photos. "You have been very helpful. We may have more questions later, but you are free to go. You can collect your pack at the front desk."

"Are you letting Martin go?"

"For now," was the comment from the other officer.

I couldn't wait to talk to Martin in the morning. That's if I survived talking with Mum and Dad tonight.

My second day at Bellfield West College, started with Dad taking me to school, even though it meant rescheduling a meeting. Maybe, he hoped to encounter Martin walking to school so he could look him over. The parents suggested I avoid him. With fingers crossed behind my back, I attested, "He hasn't done anything."

I was early, so I wandered around to wait near my homeroom. There were some wood benches around a small paved area. Surprisingly, Martin was already there, slumped on one of the benches.

"Good to see you," I said.

"Is it?" He looked up and I saw a bruise on his cheek.

"Well, yeah. How come you're early? Avoiding the Logans?"

"Perhaps."

"Did they get picked up too?"

"Yeah. They weren't kept long. Old Gill was at the police station. I reckon he spoke up for them."

"So, do you think they are into something shady – like selling drugs?" I decided to be blunt.

He stared at me. "Who mentioned drugs?"

I shrugged, not mentioning the envelope that had given me visions. "Who hit you?"

"My dad was not happy to have to come and get me. Less so when the police decided he was too drunk to drive home. How did your folks take it?"

"Better than that. They know I couldn't possibly have been mixed up in anything here."

"You should have kept away from me."

"So are you here now to avoid being at home, or for some other reason?"

"I don't know what my cousins were up to yesterday."

"Cousins...okay..."

"They were speaking to some bloke who went off when we were approaching. No one I recognized. And I am sure they were putting stuff in their pockets."

"So..."

"They either ditched stuff or didn't get searched. I was going to look around, but I reckon the police are still watching the school."

"Why are you trying to protect them?"

"That's my business."

"Okay, okay. I'm just trying to help."

Martin's expression changed from a scowl to a lop-sided grin. "I'm surprised you are still talking to me."

"Did everyone else stop talking to you when they found drugs in your locker?"

The scowl returned. "Pretty much."

"If you haven't done anything, no one can prove you did. Let the police figure things."

"I guess..."

"Um...I didn't know if you'd get a chance to clean your blazer." He still wasn't wearing one. "So I borrowed my mum's clothes brush, if you'd like to use it."

I dumped my bag and zipped open one of the outer pockets.

"You are a bossy one, aren't you?"

"You don't have to use it if you like detention."

Martin accepted the brush, and set to work on the crumpled blazer he took from his bag. By the time the next earliest people began to arrive, he had his blazer on and I'd tucked the brush back in my bag.

At morning homeroom, the only reference to the previous afternoon, was for everyone to report any strangers hanging around the school. I wondered about the two absent boys, but I was more interested in the girl who had not been present yesterday. She was sitting with Gail, and her friends. I knew, from the glances my way, that I was a topic of their covert whispering. I could guess – new girl, all her stuff is second hand, had a warning on her first day. My thought was, *Thank heavens they don't know about yesterday afternoon!*

Deliberately, I smiled in that direction, locating the new face. Abbie Carson. Our first names were similar, but I'd never be mistaken for her. She'd bleached her hair, and had it cut stylishly short. As expected, she ignored me. *Her loss!*

At first break, I sat with Naomi and her friend Karen who, uncomfortably for her, was the niece of our homeroom teacher.

"You know how Toby and Adam were absent?" Karen asked the group. "I overheard Mr Gill telling Ms Sutton that the police had picked them up yesterday with drugs on them."

She looked at me then and said, "Martin Kemple was another one they picked up."

I said, "So? He's here. They can't have found anything on him." If they didn't know about me, I wasn't going to say a word. "Was there anyone else?"

"Yes but I didn't hear who. They saw me coming to give Ms Sutton my spare locker key and stopped talking."

That was another of those little things I didn't know. Mum didn't have time yesterday to get to the post office to pick up our held mail. Now I'd need to get another key cut.

Someone must have reserved a locker for Abbie, because I discovered hers was almost above mine.

"Move out of the way, Charity Case," was her greeting.

"I won't be long." I ignored her shoving.

"It's bad enough being above smelly Kemple. Where is he by the way? I hear you have a thing for him."

When I had collected what I needed, I stood and turned to face her. "You heard wrong."

During History, I did wonder where Martin was. He was still missing at the start of Italian and by chance I saw him coming from the admin as I was returning from the library after organizing my school ID. I slowed in case he wanted to catch up. He did.

"You're a bit late for class."

"I've been in Gill's office, answering questions. He had two police guys there."

"Questions about what?"

"Lots of stuff. They found drugs on five students, and two of those claim it was me who sold it to them."

"Yesterday?"

"Yes."

"You couldn't have. I was with you after classes finished, and the police found nothing on you, didn't they?"

"No. They even ran some electronic thing over me and my stuff, and swabbed my hands with something. They might want to talk to you again."

"I can say I was with you after classes, but I can't say about earlier during breaks."

"I know that." He was worried, that was easy to see.

"Were the police also at the front of the school?"

"Dunno, why?"

I shrugged. "Just thinking...we'd better scurry back to class."

The Italian teacher had discovered I was abysmal when it came to Italian. She held me back to suggest some remedial study. It meant that I was last to the lockers. Martin though, was still fiddling in his when I knelt down at mine. He looked at me with a face that was drained of all colour.

"What's wrong?"

"Someone has put shit in here again."

He showed me an envelope, like the one I had picked up yesterday, and a fleeting touch on one edge confirmed my guess. *Drugs.*

"Someone is going to report it," Martin said, hiding the envelope again. He was being careful not to hold it.

"Can you edge it into my locker?" I asked abruptly.

"What?"

"Do it. I will hand it in later, so it will look as if someone is targeting you and got the locker wrong."

"You'll get in trouble."

"No, an advantage of being new..."

He was right though, but this was bullying taken to a new level.

While listening to my new friends planning a week-end meet-up, I had my eye on another group of my classmates. Yesterday, I had only been interested in Tom and Gerry Logan, Martin's cousins. Today, I noticed that Abbie and Helen were all over two other boys. Jackie was alone until another boy joined the group. I saw him pass her something small.

This little mystery took my mind off the way my lunch was sitting like a lump in my stomach. I was sure something nasty was afoot, aimed at Martin, and I was starting to regret my hasty decision to help him. Someone was trying to discredit him, and if my vague, unformed plan went awry, the teachers would consider me his accomplice. The yellow envelope in my locker, that had been in his, was identical to the one I had picked up yesterday. Too much of a coincidence to be unrelated.

Martin seemed to be a bit of a loner, either by choice or from his choice of deodorant. Although warned to keep clear from him, I had yet to see a reason why.

I had been considering how someone could have planted that envelope in his locker. There was no master key, since everyone supplied their own lock. All I could conclude was that someone – probably from our class – had borrowed Martin's spare key from Ms Sutton. She kept them in a pencil case that had been put in a locked drawer. The spares had students' names and locker number on a tag.

The problem with my rash plan was that I had not brought in a spare key. So, when I 'found' the envelope in my locker, if I wasn't first suspect, they would think that Martin put it there and I couldn't think of a logical alternative. Then, I was wondering when the troublemaker was going to set the teachers onto Martin. I wanted the teachers to have found nothing in his locker before I produced it.

"Are year twelves allowed to use their phones during break?"
I asked my new friends during a lull in their chatter. Jackie's
boyfriend was using his.

Naomi simply said, "No."

Karen snickered, "Jordan will hide it quickly enough if he
knew Tucker was coming."

Abbie had spotted the teacher and gestured a warning with
her head. Jordan ended the call, but it rang straight after. The
teacher's head swiveled in their direction. As he walked closer,
the phone was passed from hand to hand and the furthest
from the teacher pushed it under some bushes. The ring had
been heard, even though Jordan had silenced it at once.

My friends all heard the Logan brothers lie, saying the sound
had come from further off.

"Let's go wandering around," Karen suggested.

"I need to go somewhere anyway," Naomi said.

"What about you, Annie?" Karen asked.

"I think I'd like to explore a bit."

Even though the students on the basketball court were making
a racket, I heard Tucker telling the boys to see if they could
find the owner of the phone.

I wasn't surprised when the Logans came after me. I heard
them getting closer and decided to do an abrupt about face.
"Oh, hello! Can you tell me where the music rooms are?"

"Why don't you ask Martin?" Gerry asked blandly.

"At least, he'd tell me, but, hey, he's not here!"

"Do you have a phone?" Tom asked.

"Yeah. In my bag, in my locker."

When they had disappeared around a corner, I returned
to the raised garden bed around which that group had been
lounging. I was considering mischief, like hiding the phone in
a different place, or handing it in as lost property. That was
until I picked it up.

My mind was grabbed, so that it seemed that I was walking in

Jordan's shoes, but in reverse from the present. I was hearing him ordering more odd named things, him telling Jackie to get Martin's spare key, him hatching a plot to further discredit Martin, him selling stuff at the school – out the front amongst the milling parents and students.

I slipped the phone in my pocket after seeing there were unread messages, and went to find Karen. "How would you like to find the phone that Tucker was after?"

Her eyes lit up. "And give it to him?" I nodded and the phone went from pocket to pocket unobtrusively.

I excused myself again and went to where I could watch the door to the admin area. Jordan had been doing something just before his return, probably arranging for someone else to accuse Martin of selling drugs.

With my poor distance vision, I couldn't identify the people going in and out – except for Tucker. He had walked past me and headed there.

Just before the bell, Martin trotted up and hissed, "If they ask, say I lent you a lock for your locker." I nodded, and he went off. He must have thought of a way around that problem although I couldn't figure it.

Mr Gill was waiting with Ms Sutton when the class were at the lockers. Martin was called over, and I could picture them asking him to open his locker, once we were all out of the way. He didn't come into class, and by now all sorts of rumors were circulating about yesterday. I said nothing, for my guts were in an even tighter knot.

I joined the rush to the lockers, but I caught sight of Jackie going up to the front desk, and Ms Sutton bringing out her pencil case of spare keys. I edged in and opened my locker, and let the envelope fall out. I stared at it as if confused.

Someone asked, "What's that."

"No idea." When I pretended that I was going to open it, Naomi hissed, "Don't! Give it to Ms Sutton."

At the front, I showed Ms Sutton what I had 'innocently' found. She took it and I was told to sit down, and see her later. Jackie was white faced as I passed her on the way to the nearest empty seat.

When the bell went, Ms Sutton asked Jackie to stay back. By the tight look on her face, she had come to a conclusion that she didn't like. We both had to open our lockers. Mine was clean, but in Jackie's there was a small plastic bag containing white tablets.

We were both escorted to admin, where Ms Sutton's report bought Gill and two policemen out of his office. I caught sight of Jordan at the front office, coming to claim his phone. It had been mentioned over the speaker during Homeroom. Tucker was talking to a man in the foyer, and he nodded towards Jordan, who caught sight of Jackie and turned abruptly to leave. The stranger grabbed him and I was sure I heard the click of handcuffs.

I hoped Jackie had the sense to tell all she knew. She was a victim, and needed help. Jordan, I decided, had been plain stupid. Perhaps my version of the truth wouldn't be needed.

I had only needed to confirm the time I had arrived that morning and found Martin there.

Ms Sutton's arrival had both sparked and quenched the idea that Martin had deliberately hidden the stuff in my locker. She'd had the spare keys with her overnight, unintentionally, and returned it to its keeping place at morning homeroom and only Jackie had come near it to get her spare key. When she returned it, Ms Sutton had known of the claim against Martin, and then I had found and reported the envelope in my locker.

At that point, it was obvious that Martin was being set up.

Jackie broke down and told all she knew. Jordan had asked her to get the key for Martin's locker. From last year, she knew his tag. She had passed it on, and later returned it. She had known what Jordan and his two mates, the boys Abbie and Helen had been with, were doing, but he was giving her tablets to help her deal with stress. For Martin's sake, I was relieved that his cousins had been hangers on and occasional unwitting messengers.

When we were finally allowed to go home, Martin shared a few details that I had not been privy to.

"Jordan sent his younger brother to claim that I had been selling stuff out the front before school started, and I had moved off when the duty teacher arrived." Martin said. "Your turning up early – well, they wouldn't have expected that. Gill will probably talk to your parents to confirm it."

I shrugged. "Dad will know when he dropped me off. I gather they checked your locker..."

"And searched me and my bag," Martin said. "Gill kept me in his office until the police arrived. They wanted to know what I had done with the rest of the stuff and the money. You should have seen Gill's face when Sutton came in and told them what you had found in your locker."

"I didn't have to say you'd lent me a lock, thankfully. I couldn't see how that would help. You might still have had a spare key."

"Oh, they thought that until Sutton mentioned Jackie borrowing her spare and returning it."

"I don't understand how you got around that."

Martin laughed briefly. "I have a unique key tag. Anyone who has been in my class before would probably recognize it. I told them that I had lent you that lock, and I had used an old one that I'd used on my bike and which only had one key."

"Devious," I commended. "No wonder Jackie nearly fainted when she saw what I had. She must have thought she had given Jordan the wrong key. I will tell you though, that my guts were in knots."

"I would have been in bad if you hadn't helped me and I don't think that it occurred to anyone that you would – no one else would have."

"So your cousins were only messengers?"

"Seems so, and if not, I hope this scares sense into them." He sighed.

"What?"

"Their step father will still probably blame me for leading them into trouble."

"But you didn't."

"No, but the guy doesn't like me, or my Dad."

"How come?"

"Just reasons. Nothing you can do about it, so there's no need to know. What I do want to know is how you figured out that Jordan was involved and got his phone. The idiot kept messages on there from the guy who was supplying him."

I recounted the incident at lunch.

Martin laughed again. "He certainly didn't count on you! But still, how did you know?"

I echoed Martin's words, "You don't need to know."

I'd better watch myself, I decided. My freaky gift was likely to get me in trouble, and I had only been at Bellfield College two days.

# Episode 2

## Friend or Unfriend?
### (Annie's POV)

### Chapter 1

"We're going to be late," Martin Kemple stated, as he lay at the kerb edge of the nature strip with one arm down the drain. "I can't feel anything down here."

Maybe he couldn't, but the yapping was frantic and I couldn't just walk away. "Let me try."

"Do you like detention?" he called back over his shoulder, reminding me of the question I'd asked him last week. "My arm is longer and I am already dusty. Maybe we should get the council ranger out here?"

"No!"

"You aren't thinking of keeping it if we actually can get it out? What would you do with it during classes?"

"I'll think of something!" Nothing sprang to mind immediately, however.

The yapping stopped a microsecond before Martin yelled, "Ow! The little bastard has my finger."

"Then bring it out...carefully." I mentally willed the poor thing to hang on, and began to dig in my bag for the hand towel I had there for PE.

The bedraggled creature was barely as long as my hand. As I wrapped the puppy in the towel, Martin gently released its grip.

I looked at Martin. "How's the finger?"

"Lucky its teeth are still tiny. It didn't draw blood." He quickly put his blazer back on and hefted his school backpack on his shoulders. "I'll hold that little carnivore while you get your bag on."

Martin gently rubbed it while I did, and then looked to see what sex it was. "A female! That would be right. And hardly weaned. You can have it."

I held it close to me as we hurried to make up time in getting to school. I wished I dare keep it in my blazer pocket, but there was no chance of that. I would have to leave it alone during PE for a start. No better ideas had occurred to me when we arrived at the back gate. The first bell had just rung.

"I have an idea," Martin told me. "Give it to me and I'll catch up."

"What?"

"Tell you later. Get to class."

I had no reason not to trust Martin, but he'd be in more trouble if he were late. I went, but I looked back to see where he went and he had disappeared. Like he seemed to do at every break. We were friends of a sort, but only when going to and from school, it seemed.

Martin arrived, panting slightly, just before Ms Sutton marked him late or absent. However, there was no time to ask him where the pup was, as I had to get to Maths, which, now that I had been put in with the year 11s, was not in the homeroom.

The route I chose to get to the other classroom was outside, and my mind was still on the question of where the pup was. Even as I was settling in a seat half way down the room, I was paying little attention to the strangers I was with. Not surprising, I jumped when I heard a voice I knew.

"What were you and Kemple up to together that you both arrived late and out of breath?"

"Trying not to be late," I retorted quietly. "How come you're here?" I didn't really fancy Abbie Carson's company. She and her friends had been a pack of sourpusses for the past week. Now, she was not scowling, but only because she was out to rile me.

"Figure it out, Charity Case."

"You must be as good as I am at maths, then," I grinned.

Abbie and her friends thought they were better than I was because they didn't have second hand stuff. She'd got my subtle put down, and the scowl was back. She didn't have to sit near me, but I wasn't going to tell her that. I didn't know anyone in this class yet, neither did she.

My patience and tolerance were at a very low ebb by the end of that double period. Abbie kept murmuring dire warnings about Martin getting what he deserved. My jaw was aching with my determination not to react to her jibes. Her boyfriend, and Helen's, had been suspended indefinitely, because they had been abetting their friend Jordan in selling drugs at the school. They had tried to make it seem that Martin was the ringleader. I wondered how much she cared for Jackie, one of her friends, who had become addicted to something thanks to the now expelled Jordan. If she learnt my part in finding the truth, she would be a hundred times worse.

Martin was hovering when I returned to my locker. Abbie glanced from him to me and smirked. Not wanting to give her any more lewd ideas about us, I caught Martin's eye, and walked away from him. Somehow he realized my intention, and met me around the back of the classrooms.

"Come with me," he said, and moved off towards where they kept the wheeled rubbish bins during the week.

I followed, full of curiosity, and when I caught up to him I asked, "Where are we going." There were still parts of the school I hadn't seen.

"One of the gardeners is a friend of mine. He's minding the pup."

The shed door was open and very faintly, I heard the puppy yapping. Martin introduced me to Ivan, who pointed to a box in one corner.

"I gave the critter some milk and cooled soup. It has slept

most of the morning, poor little thing."

The puppy sounded happier now, and I went to pick it up. This time, the towel was not around it and it wriggled and tried to lick me. For once, the funny talent I had for sensing the recent past of objects, gave me a sense of delight and joy, but it didn't last. As the past unraveled in reverse, I had the feel of terror as the pup had been in water, paddling for its life to stay afloat, after having been separated from its litter mates. Before that there had been the sense of nearly suffocating in a dark place, squashed on all sides by other puppy bodies.

"What's the matter?" Martin asked. He must have seen the tears I tried to wipe away.

"I am happy we saved this pup, but I wonder if others were down in the drain."

"Hmm," was all Martin said. "I will check on her at lunch and bring her out to you at the gate after classes, okay. We are not meant to be here."


PE was next, and we were to have our fitness levels tested. That was something new and I was looking forward to it. Until I came back to change into my sport uniform and found that someone had taken my shoes from my drawstring carry bag. I'd only been away a couple of minutes. No one seemed to be watching for my reaction, but it had to be Abbie or one of her friends. They were in a huddle chuckling, as I looked around for where they might have been put. I couldn't look in their fancy sport bags. *What could I do?*

With a second uniform warning in two weeks, neither really being my fault, I was in a foul mood. Heaven help whoever had pinched my shoes.

At least this PE session was being held on the mezzanine level of the auditorium where the basketball courts were. Socked feet were not unpleasant, in fact some of the boys also removed their shoes. Abbie and Gail were taking turns to needle me, and occasionally shoving me. Once I had fallen onto some of the equipment and been told to be more careful. From then on, I was waiting for my chance.

The waft of their deodorant gave me a second's warning and I turned abruptly and grabbed Abbie's outstretched arm, just before it shoved me, and pulled her off balance.

I stopped her falling over. "Sorry! But you really shouldn't walk so close behind a person." My smirk, told her I had known they were there. She was rubbing her shoulder; my yank hadn't been gentle.

"I'll get you for that," she muttered, moving away.

She was lucky that was all I did, but I was sure that the teacher would not be impressed if I did a judo throw with her. For the rest of the period, I managed to keep with my friends. Most of us weren't rushing to change back into our normal uniform, since it was lunch break, but I got dressed quickly, because I wanted a chance to try and find my shoes. Surely they must be in the change room somewhere.

I was checking the cubicles in the girls' toilets, when I heard one of the teachers talking to Naomi, who was waiting for me. Having no luck, I returned to get my stuff and head to lunch.

"Annie, a word with you," the teacher, one who had supervised the PE session, directed quietly.

I walked over to her, and sensed Naomi moving out of earshot.

"I know you couldn't find your shoes earlier, but can you explain how they got into the equipment room?"

"Where's that?"

"Don't you know?"

"Except for the assembly on the first day, this is only the second time I have been in this building," I explained, guessing the teacher wasn't aware I was a new student.

"I see. Then who might have wanted you in trouble? Abbie and Helen?"

I wasn't quite sure what to say. If I got them in trouble, they'd be worse.

"I can't think why they would. However, they've been grumpy for the past week. Still, why would they take it out on me?"

I had a fair idea why, but I hadn't been talking about my part in proving Martin innocent, and their boyfriends guilty.

The teacher sighed, and said, "You can pick them up from Admin after classes."

"Thank you. What about the uniform warning? Since it wasn't my fault?"

"You will have them for the next session, so it shouldn't be a problem. Just keep a better eye on them."

When the teacher had gone, Naomi came over. She'd heard the conversation. "It had to be Abbie, or rather her idea. She and Gail barged into the space between your stuff and mine. Helen or Clare could've done it."

I thought on that while we walked towards our lockers. Finally, I decided, "Forget it. They are petty minded idiots!"

"Abbie holds grudges. What might you have done to annoy her?"

"Her boyfriend and Jordan, tried to convince everyone that Martin was early to school Tuesday last week, selling drugs at the front of the school. Only thing was, I was early too, and we were both waiting for the bell near our homeroom."

"Abbie had a thing for Martin in year 7," Naomi said. "She

says he dumped her… might have been the other way round."

"Maybe. He isn't particularly well off."

"What's it with you and Martin?"

"What's what?"

"You know. He talks to you, hardly anyone else."

"I met him while walking to school on my first day. He seems friendlier outside of school, I will admit." That reminded me of the puppy in the gardener's shed. I wanted to see her even though Martin had said he'd check on her.

"Let's get our lunch," Naomi suggested.

Halfway through the break, I excused myself and headed, in a roundabout way to the gardener's shed. I had seen Martin at a distance, and it seemed he was heading that way. My route took me behind the music prac rooms, out of sight of most students and the patrolling teachers. If I had thought of it, I should have looked out for Abbie, since I had noticed that she wasn't with her usual group of cronies. I was startled when she stepped out in front of me.

"Going to meet Kemple, are you Jamieson?" she taunted. "You're about as subtle as a brick through a window, you know."

"I hope you weren't going out to meet your druggie boyfriend, Carson!"

I shouldn't have said it, but I'd had enough of her, and at least here, no one was watching us. I went on. "And your little practical joke with the shoes backfired. Yes, I got a warning, but they revoked it when they realized that I had no way of knowing the place where you put them."

"I didn't touch them!"

"No, that's right, you got Helen to do your dirty work."

From her expression, mouth dropping open before being snapped shut, I had guessed right.

"You bitch. I know you helped get Adam in trouble."

"So that's the bee in your knickers," I told her. "I didn't make him help sell drugs to kids. You should thank your lucky stars he didn't get you addicted, like Jordan did to Jackie."

That was too much. Abbie flung herself at me, fingers curled into talons, trying to scratch. This time I did what I had resisted during PE. A quick twist and kick and she was on her rump on the dirt. She didn't stay down, she was furious. Her next try was to kick me, but I jumped back, then charged her, repeating the same move I had done before.

A distraction in the form of a hand sized tan puppy, allowed her to close and grab my hair. She yanked and laughed. She didn't notice or care about the dog. However, when I had been taught self-defence, my teacher had taught me what to do when that tempting target was taken.

Abbie was red faced, and cursing me with words I hadn't expected her to know. I grabbed the puppy before she hit it in spite. She still wasn't giving up, and came at me again. I had to put the tiny dog in my blazer pocket, to protect it. I had a glimpse of Martin trotting up the path from the shed, and then ducking out of sight. The reason was obvious. The on-duty teacher ran up and pulled us apart.

Most of what was said was lost as the blood pounded in my ears. Abbie was busy trying to wriggle out by blaming me, but her claims were ignored. We were to go to Admin and wait for Mr Gill.

My face was so hot it must be glowing. I had never been in trouble before, but felt the Acting Headmaster thought me a habitual trouble maker. I wasn't, but was I to just stand around and let Abbie hit on me?

"Now, what was this fight about?" Gill demanded. I glanced up, he was looking at me.

"I don't know exactly."

"It wasn't that you thought Miss Carson took your shoes earlier?"

"No, Sir. I didn't know who did that."

"What about you Miss Carson? Do you know what this fight was about?"

She wasn't going to admit she started it...

"She shoved me in PE and jerked my shoulder," Abbie said, picking the one truth that made me look bad.

"Did you?" Gill demanded of me.

Two could play that game. "She was right behind me when I suddenly turned around. She was off balance and I stopped her falling over."

"So why were you both behind the prac rooms?"

"Sir, I went to warn her that we aren't meant to be there," Abbie said at once.

Gill looked at me.

"I am still learning my way around."

"And how did this fight start, if each of you had innocent intentions?"

"She saw me and came at me," Abbie said. "She must have thought I meant to get back at her for jerking my arm."

My turn. "Abbie stepped out in front of me, and came at me. I reacted and she ended up on her rump. That made her angry and by then I had had enough of her needling me all morning."

I decided that I might as well admit all of it.

"You liar! You started it!" Abbie yelled.

"Silence!" Gill's expression was unforgiving. "Neither of you should have been fighting."

I felt the puppy starting to wriggle in my pocket, and then it began yipping.

"What is that in your pocket?"

I had been keeping my hand there, and the puppy had been happily licking it. I obeyed the implied order, and lifted it out.

"There is a rule against bringing pets to school. Where you aware of that, Miss Jamieson?"

"We found it on the way to school."

"We?" Gill looked from Abbie to me and back.

"Not me," Abbie proclaimed putting her hands up as if to say she hadn't touched the dog.

"Martin Kemple and me. It was down a drain, and frantic."

"You should have rung the council ranger."

"We didn't have the number, and how soon would they have come? We couldn't wait for them to decide, and by then this little pup might have been dead. She was exhausted and hardly breathing when Martin got her out." All that burst out of me, and I added, "What if there had been others and this was the only one still alive? We couldn't let it die too. And the only reason we brought it here was that we were starting to run late for school."

Gill's expression had softened, but only a little. "Where has it been all morning?"

"One of the gardeners offered to look after it – but it must have got free."

"What were you going to do?"

"Just check on it. I don't know if I'll be able to keep it, but I feel responsible for it."

Gill considered us both for a while.

"Can I be assured that the pair of you will acted like civilized young women from now on?"

We both gave the affirmative answer we knew he expected.

"Then sit down outside my office while I decide what to do with you."

Gill went off, leaving us glaring at each other. There was a lot I wanted to say to Abbie Carson, but outside Gill's office was not a good place to say it. So I turned my attention to the pup, and let it out of my pocket and onto my lap. Stroking it helped me calm down.

"I still don't like you!" Abbie announced, but her voice was low.

"You don't have to," I told her. "We don't have to be friends and I really don't care what you think of me. Just leave me alone!"

After that, we sat in silence, and I let the puppy loose on the empty seat between us. I didn't mind when it went to sniff Abbie, and she gently patted it. I was surprised when she said, "If it had been me, I'd have done the same. Tried to save it. Do you really think there might have been more chucked down there?"

"Yes." I wasn't going to mention what my mind had pictured when I first held the pup.

"Have you given her a name?"

"I thought about calling her 'Lucky'."

Gill returned, just as the pup yipped, as if agreeing.

Ivan was with him, and I allowed him to take the pup. She didn't object, so long as she was getting attention, and she no doubt recalled he had fed her.


"My office, ladies," Gill invited. Abbie and I exchanged glances.

"I have decided, that the two of you have not had a chance to get to know each other. It led me to recall some advice I heard when I was much your age. 'You never stood in that man's shoes, or saw things through his eyes. So before you abuse, criticize and accuse, walk a mile in his shoes.' I want you both to make a list of ten things that are good about the other, and I want to have it on my desk first thing tomorrow."

"Yes, Sir." Abbie and I echoed each other.

"I will have a letter for each of you to take home. You are to meet me here directly after home room."

There wasn't much of the break left, and I was as glad to escape as Abbie probably was. We each went off in different directions. I went around to near our homeroom, since I didn't really want to talk to anyone just then.

I didn't mind it when Martin turned up. I had to grin when he commented, "Well, he didn't tar and feather you...so what did he say?"

"Lots that I prefer to forget," I said.

"Did he give you detention?"

"No." I explained what Gill had said we were to do.

"Quoting Elvis Presley was he? The guy has been dead forty years. There has to be a catch. Gill doesn't play nice. If it had been me, I'd have been suspended for a week."

"He mentioned a letter to go home..."

"Yeah, that's normal."

He drifted off when the bell went, leaving me with a shivery feeling. Did Gill have something else in mind?

He did, as I discovered after retrieving my sport shoes after class.

"You have to be joking! My father will never allow this," Abbie argued. "These are expensive orthopaedic sport shoes - made to fit my feet. They'll be ruined if someone else walks in them."

My father would laugh. However, the idea made me go pale. Wearing Abbie's shoes was likely to show me more than I cared to about her, and probably wouldn't help me find ten things to like about her.

I stayed quiet. Gill had decided. That was that.

"The option is a three day suspension."

Now, Abbie went pale.

I'd had enough of Abbie's 'expensive orthopaedic shoes' by the time I had reached the back gate. I was getting flashes of Abbie's life. By concentrating on my uncomfortable feet and the puppy, I was keeping them at bay. As soon as I was a block away from school, I changed into my own black school shoes.

*Was Abbie doing the same on the school bus?*

Martin had laughed when I told him of Gill's punishment. Except for one aspect. I thought it would punish Abbie worse than me. So it should, she started it.

My parents would begin to wonder if they had chosen the right school for me. I had never been in trouble before this.

"What if your parents won't let you keep the puppy?" Martin asked.

"It's more whether the property owner will allow pets. Would you be able to?"

"Not a good idea, although I would love to. I do have bowls and stuff from when we did have a dog, if you want."

"I will let you know. Do you want my phone number?"

"Ok. You can have mine if you want."

At home, I put the pup in Mum's empty clothes basket. It was plastic and about the size of a baby's bath and just high enough to contain her. For company, I found my tattiest teddy bear and a ticking clock. After giving her a saucer of made up gravy mix, she settled to sleep. I went to get tea started.

When my Dad got home, she was awake and being the welcoming committee.

"Annie?"

"Yes, Dad?"

"Why is there a dog in the laundry?"

"Oh, um, well... Martin and I rescued her from a drain this

morning. Can we keep her? Pleeeese?"

If I thought the pup would distract him from the envelope I had put on the hall table...I thought again. He was frowning at the school emblem on the envelope.

"Do I want to read this?" he had his brows raised now, and looking at me.

I wanted to squirm. "Um, not really..."

"Then bring me a cold drink and we can sit and you can tell me about your day."

So I did. That's what I liked about my Dad, he'd listen to me and try to understand my side of things. I've never tried to hide anything from him...well, except for the images I got from things. That was way out of his understanding.

As I expected, Mr Gill's novel punishment made him laugh. It didn't stop him telling me to mind my 'annoyance' in future.

"I know she's in a snit because of last week. Her boyfriend has been warned to stay away from her. Her friends are just as sulky, but why take it out on me? Just because I stood up for Martin. Their friends were trying to frame him. That wasn't fair."

"No," my Dad agreed. "But some people have to try to make others miserable when they are."

"Well, it's not as if she were the first person to be dumped," I muttered. "I haven't heard from Colin since the last day of last term. He promised he'd call me to see how we were going."

Dad distracted me by saying, "Kiddo, I will ask about the pup, but no promises."


My Mum let me move Lucky Pup into my bedroom while I did homework. She inspired one item for my Abbie list – Abbie cares about animals.

The only other thing to come to mind was – she is always impeccably groomed...*until I started pulling her hair...*

Then I added, 'Abbie is lucky'. Her parents give her lots of money and anything she wants. That wouldn't go down well with Gill, so I added, 'She was not made into an addict.'

My mind was a blank then, so I went onto other work and hoped other ideas would emerge. Touching Abbie's shoes again would be a desperate last resort. Gill was right. We really didn't know each other. He certainly can't have known of my mind trick on receiving from objects, so why had he decided on a shoe swap?

When I came back to the list, I added, 'Abbie is loyal to her friends.' I didn't add they were a bunch of snobs.

What else? Maths! Yes. 'Abbie is good at maths, like me.' Half way there. I was stuck.

With reluctance, I reached into my bag for one of the bright green-laced Nike shoes. I sat back then, and let the images flow. In a way, this was like I was peeking in someone's window.

While I had been ignoring the flashing images earlier, events of that day must have passed by. For what I began seeing now was Abbie walking around a huge, elegant house. Her parents must be really rich if they could afford an indoor Jacuzzi.

It took me a while to realise that Abbie was alone, I saw no other people. Perhaps though, both her parents were at work. Time continued backwards, to some earlier night time.

For meals, she was eating from cans. To sleep, she locked her bedroom door and curled up in a chair with her iPod playing music. What was going on? Where were her parents? The answer came in time. First, an image of Abbie listening to a phone message. Someone called Nancy – apologising for not being able to work for a while due to a family emergency. Then an image of Abbie's parents. They were going away for business, and Nancy would be looking after her. The Nancy who couldn't come?

I dropped the shoe. Abbie was on her own, in that big house? That couldn't be right. I touched the shoe again. Now her parents were giving her a long list of instructions. Don't open the door to strangers, don't tell anyone we aren't here, don't mention our business to anyone, if she needed to call, use her mum's mobile number, and don't try to call the hotel.

Compared to my parents, Abbie's seemed to be acting oddly. That thought seemed to bring out the events of last week, when they had been asked to come to the school. Her father had rushed off, for some reason.

I shivered, thinking of Abbie being all on her own for the past week. No wonder she went pale at the option of a three day suspension. Gill would want to talk to her parents…

On my list I jotted down, "Abbie likes that same music as I do. Abbie is obedient to her parents' wishes. She does her homework without being nagged, and is brave when her parents are away and she only has a servant to be with her."

How could I hate Abbie, when her life was so lonely? Had her parents even rung to check she was okay? Or answered the text messages she was sending?

Abbie needed help, but what could I do that wouldn't make things worse? She probably hadn't even told her friends. I only knew from my odd talent, and my parents blamed that on an overactive imagination. I couldn't even ask Abbie if the things I had seen were true.

Maybe succumbing to seeing the images that came to my mind when holding Abbie's shoes had been a bad idea. Mr Gill had only commented, when he had glanced through our lists of what we'd discovered about each other, that neither of us had reached ten things. He had given each of us the other's list. I'd shoved it straight into a pocket, aware that it was almost time for homeroom. Abbie had done the same.

Neither of us spoke a word once we left the Acting Headmaster and begun trotting to our homeroom. Abbie sought the comfort of her friends. I slipped into an empty seat near the back, but one where I could watch her. She surreptitiously opened up the sheet of paper I had written my list on – I had used pale pink paper. It seemed her friends wanted to read it, but she folded it again, quickly, and hid it. She gestured at Ms Sutton, probably as her reason.

I wasn't sure that I wanted to read what Abbie had said about me. In fact, I put it out of my mind until she cornered me at the first break. The only reason that I didn't walk off to avoid her was that she was alone.

"Have you been spying on me?" she demanded from three feet away.

"No."

"You must have been! How else could you know half the stuff you wrote?"

"I don't know where you live, and I haven't been interested in you or your friends since the brush off Gail gave me on day one."

Abbie's frown turned to more of a scowl. "It's not true, you know."

If she wanted me to forget what she had just accused me of, I could. "Don't tell Gill, huh? I just held your shoes and jotted down what I thought of when trying to imagine I was you."

"Well, don't start spreading those rumours around, Jamieson." She turned and stalked off.

*Wouldn't dream of implying you weren't human!*

While I was alone, I took out her list and read, "We wear the same size shoes. She doesn't care if her clothes aren't new. She'll try making friends with anyone. She likes dogs. She must be good at maths, too."

I could just imagine the sneer in her tone if she was reading it to her friends. I shrugged and went to find those who were my friends.


I was getting my books for the next period when I was jostled by Gail and Clare. I doubted that it was accidental.

I heard, "What did you do to upset Abbie?"

"Nothing," was pretty much the truth as far as I knew.

"Well you keep away from her! She doesn't need more grief from you."

*Bitches!* "Then you suggest to her that she switches lockers. Otherwise, she will have to come near me."

I locked my locker and stood up while they were deciding if I had insulted one of them. They shoved me hard, but I fell against Martin, not the lockers. Gail smirked and walked off with Clare.

"Are those bitches at it again?" I heard Martin's low voice.

"It's not important," I assured him in a similarly low voice.

We separated, me to Italian, Martin to Japanese, and Abbie's friends to textiles.

My promise to myself that I would try harder in Italian didn't work. I was irritated by Gail's attitude and perversely, worried about Abbie, who must be bottling stuff up inside her, and not even telling her friends. I didn't know how to help – if what I had envisioned was fact. No one would believe me. Even Mum and Dad said that the things I claimed to have seen were merely my imagination.

Trouble was, this getting of images while handling objects was getting more frequent and at times it was distracting. Was there anyone who could tell me how to control it? Maybe I could look on the internet during the lunch break. We were allowed to use the computers then.

During the rest of Italian, and the following hour of History, I thought of a few things to check on, and I also decided to start a diary of what I saw from objects. That way, maybe, I could discover how many were true.

Before the library got busy, I picked the end most computer, in the most remote section of the library, and turned the screen slightly away from the next nearest computer to my right.

Firstly, I discovered that what I had was referred to as psychometry. At best it was a pseudo-science and at worst considered absolute bunkum. The sites I looked at were iffy at best, so I turned my attention to seeing if I could find anything about Abbie's parents. A waste of time, since I didn't even know their names.

I had just cleared the screen, and was considering going outside, when someone pulled up a chair between me and the wall.

*Abbie? What the hell...* I glanced around, in case Gail, Clare and Helen were following.

I waited for her to speak, but she was hugging some books to her chest, and biting her lip.

"Well?"

"I wanted to show you something."

"Okay..."

Like a conjurer, she slipped a brochure from between two books and placed it in from of me. It was for some kind of time-share thing, and it meant nothing to me.

"So?" I wasn't going to touch it.

"Look, I don't know how you guessed so much about me, and

I reckon just touching something of mine is rubbish, but..."

I got it. She didn't believe my claim, but she wanted to know something. *Was I about to become the laughing stock of the school?*

Slowly, I moved to take the brochure, and at first, I got nothing. Just as I was about to put it down, the images began. Abbie had taken it from her design teacher, who had claimed she had got it from her father, who she had recognized at some meeting last week.

"Well?" Abbie hissed.

I held up my hand. What I was receiving then was more emotion than image related to that brochure. It seemed like anger, nausea and the sense of having done something foolish.

"Did your teacher give you this?"

Abbie looked away. "Not exactly, but I will be taking it back."

"Did she tell you anything?"

"Only that my Dad had talked to her about it and she wanted to get in contact with him. I said I would see if I could contact him during lunch."

"That's what I sensed." I was biting my lip now.

"What else?" Abbie insisted.

"I just got the feeling – I think from the teacher – maybe she felt she had been scammed."

"No! You're wrong. She's wrong. My Dad wouldn't do that."

Abbie grabbed the brochure, and hid it again. Her face though, was frowning as if she was connecting unpleasant ideas.

"Don't tell anyone about this, Jamieson!"

"I won't," I assured Abbie's retreating figure. I hoped she wouldn't either.

"Do you think Abbie had a fight with the others in Gail's crowd?" Martin asked as we moved away from the rest of the class, and began to head for the school's back gate. "She didn't look happy."

"Can't say," I told him, feeling reticent. Usually, that was Martin's state.

The fact was, I was worried about Abbie, even if we weren't friends. When I'd held her shoes, I'd had a glimpse into her life which I had promised not to mention, and didn't want to be called crazy if I did.

While the rest of the class was streaming towards the front of the school to the buses or parent pick up, we were walking to the school's back entrance. I wanted to hurry home to Lucky Pup, hoping that she hadn't made a mess of the house during the day.

Martin turned suddenly and muttered, "What does she want?"

Looking to see who he meant, I saw Abbie running to catch up to us.

"Let's keep walking," Martin suggested.

"No, she's alone. Maybe she wants to be friends."

"It would be a first."

"Maybe so, but perhaps she doesn't know how to ask?"

"You had no trouble," Martin reminded me.

"I didn't ask."

When Abbie reached us, I noticed her still reddened eyes.

"I thought you usually caught the bus," Martin greeted her.

Abbie ignored him, and spoke to me. "I wanted to know how the pup was."

"She was fine this morning," I said. "Mum was going to put her in the laundry before she left for work. I am hoping I don't have another mess to clean up.”

Abbie managed a sick laugh, but made no move to go off.

I had the urge to say, “Do you want to come and see her?”

Abbie nodded. Beyond her I saw Martin scowl before blanking his expression. “How will you get home,” he asked neutrally. “We live in the opposite direction to you.”

“I’ll walk,” she sounded almost like herself.

“Or I can ask Dad to drive you home,” I countered. “You’ll let your folks know where you are....”

“It will be okay with them. They’ll both be getting home late.”

I saw Martin’s puzzled look. Did he think she was lying? I knew she was.

“Why don’t you come too, Martin? See how she likes that roly-poly toy you brought around yesterday?”

“Okay,” he agreed as we walked on in an awkward silence.

I wasn’t going to ask Abbie the questions in my mind, and she didn’t seem inclined to talk around Martin.

At home, I took them around the back. Lucky Pup must have heard us, for she was now yapping frantically. When I let her out, she ran like a dervish around our legs. I managed to catch her and give her a cuddle, but only until she could wriggle onto the next person – Martin. Then, before he could say, “She likes me,” the dervish had wriggled towards Abbie.

“I hope you can hold her. I don’t want her running outside and I need to clean up a mess.”

As I began to pick up damp newspaper, Martin said quietly, “I need to get home. Can I come another day?”

I nodded, and he gave Abbie a glance before leaving.

Abbie was smiling as the pup kept trying to lick her face. It seemed that she had forgotten whatever had upset her.

“Annie?”

“I’m in the laundry, Dad. Lucky Pup made a mess.”

I emerged from there to see my Dad giving Abbie an odd

look. "Hi Dad, meet Abbie. Can she stay for tea?"

"I suppose so. If it is okay with her parents." Now he gave me an enquiring glance, having recognized the name of my adversary of the day before. I shrugged.

"I'll ring Mum, Mr Jamieson," Abbie said quickly, giving me a look that I hoped was gratitude. Lucky Pup began squirming to get to the new arrival.

"I see yon pup has made another conquest," my dad said, as an excuse to study Abbie. I took the comment as an oblique way of asking, "How come you are friends now?"

Well, he was right. Lucky Pup had helped. "Yeah, the little traitor. Now she wants to get to you. Did I tell you, Dad, that Abbie is also doing advanced Maths? I thought we could do our homework together, and then we could drive her home?"

Abbie gave the pup to my dad, who was immediately distracted. She sidled closer to me.

"I really shouldn't stay out too late. If my parents call and I don't answer, they may get worried."

"Won't they call your mobile?"

"They don't, usually."

"Well, why don't you call them?"

The question was reasonable, even though I knew her parents hadn't answered any of her calls or texts.

Abbie took out her phone, checked for messages, then pressed one hot key. I heard it dialling, ringing and then go to message bank. Abbie left her message, then ended the call. She looked at me as if daring me to say anything.

Part of me wanted to. It didn't seem right that Abbie should be all alone in the big house I had seen in my vision. Yet, we were the same age and I was perfectly able to come home to an empty house, let myself in, start tea and mind myself until either or both of my folks got home from work.

It was just...that sensing of how things were, that had come when I touched Abbie's shoes. So, I was doing what I could, inviting her here, and asking her to tea. At least tonight she'd have a decent meal and company for a while.

Abbie's phone rang, and I saw a look of relief cross her face. I took Lucky Pup from my dad, so he could go and change from his suit, and went to finish putting clean paper down in the laundry. The pup wanted to play, but I put her in the basket and promised her food as soon as I could. I wasn't going to eavesdrop on Abbie's call.

She came into the kitchen when I was peeling potatoes. "Everything okay?"

"Yeah. I told mum that Mrs Hanson had to go off on a family emergency, but I'd be okay on my own for tonight. That I was at a friends and would be driven home. They'll be coming back tomorrow."

*I was her friend now? Okay....*

"Want to help?" I pointed to the carrots I hadn't got to peeling yet.

"No. At home, Mrs Hanson does that."

"Lucky you! If I want tea at a decent hour, I usually start preparing it. Mum won't be home until seven-thirty tonight. She's on afternoons this week."

Some of Abbie's superior attitude had returned, but without her other friends, she was not so bad.


Her house was dark when we stopped outside, although I thought I had seen a light on in one window as we approached.

Dad remarked on the lack of lights but Abbie said, "They have an early start tomorrow. I have my own keys to get in."

As I handed Abbie her schoolbag, I had more flashes of her life. I knew she'd just lied to my dad, and she'd lied to me. Her parents weren't coming back tomorrow, and they'd been angry with her. But, perhaps the housekeeper was back.

And maybe we can talk tomorrow...or not.

# Episode 3

# Bones of an Old Mystery
## (Annie's POV)

### Chapter 1

"Do you have a plastic bag for that?" Martin asked me.

"Huh?"

"It's the law."

"What is?"

"Picking up after your dog. That's what the kiddie shovel and plastic bags that I gave you are for."

I looked down and saw what Lucky-pup had just done. "Yuk!"

He laughed. "Wait here. I'll duck back home and get something."

During the short wait, Lucky-pup kept straining her leash and trying to sniff all the new smells. I figured that there must be quite a few, ah, traps, around my backyard. That part of dog owning had never occurred to me.

When Martin returned, in less than ten minutes, he had one of those bags you get fruit and vegetables in.

Handing it to me, he was grinning. "You might as well get used to it."

"Yeah." I knew I was pulling a face as my bag-gloved hand set to work. At least it wasn't a big pile. "Now what?" I asked as I inverted the bag and tied it off.

"Well...I could think of a few places to leave it. Girls are such wusses about a little—"

"Maybe we are, but I don't want to carry this around all day."

"Ok. There's a rubbish bin near the milk bar," he decided to tell me.

It was Saturday morning and he had offered to show me around the neighbourhood – places away from the route to school or the big shopping centre. It was a good reason to get out and give Lucky-pup some exercise too.

"Seems like being human proved too much for Abbie, since she wasn't at school yesterday."

"We'll have to wait and see, won't we?"

"I predict, that by Monday, she'll be back to her usual self."

"She's got things on her mind," I found myself defending her.

"She confide in you? That'd be a first."

"Not exactly. I heard stuff."

"Yeah, but it's not as if she's the only one with problems at home. Why take it out on us?"

Martin took a ball out of his pocket and bounced it. Lucky-pup jumped up and tried to catch it. I recalled how Martin's father had been the one time I had seen him. I was lucky with my Mum and Dad.

To change the subject, I asked, "Are we going anywhere in particular?"

"Oh, the milk bar but Helen, Gail and Clare tend to hang out there. Boy watching. Then there's a short strip of shops a few streets over. There is a small cinema there that is still operating. Thought we could come back by the swimming pool. Or we could go down to River Park and walk there."

"Sounds okay, even if I will probably have to carry Lucky-pup by then."

The suburb was considered 'elite', with lots of expensive homes mostly nearer the river. However not all of the suburb was like that. Where my Dad was renting was in an area where some of the old mansions had been removed and the land used for cheaper housing – decades ago. Being a builder and architect, my father picked up trivia like that. River Park was like a buffer zone between old and new.

I shouted Martin a can of Pepsi at the milk bar and got a bottle of water for myself. We'd have stayed there longer but the 'Hell's Angels' as Martin had nicknamed Gail and her group, rode up on their bikes. It was difficult not to laugh – the name was so appropriate. Just thinking about it, made their slurs of 'Charity Case' and 'stray mutts' seem like idle chatter.

We walked on until we got around a corner, where I stopped to give Lucky-pup a drink from my palm. Her pink tongue tickled.

"I wonder what's going on up there," Martin remarked.

I stood up and dried my dog-licked palm on my jeans. "What's there?"

"An old house that has been empty for ages."

"Some of the people look like scouts. Maybe they are cleaning the place up."

Without discussing it, we began to walk that way.


"Annie!"

I heard my name called and saw Naomi trotting towards me in a scout uniform.

"Hi, what's going on?"

"Oh, we've been given this place to use as a scout hall but it's a right mess. The inside looks like a magpie's nest. Not only that, the yard's been used as a hard waste dump."

Lucky-pup began to sniff Naomi and then put her front paws on her legs.

"The little traitor wants to be fussed over," Martin drawled. He surprised Naomi just by speaking. She hid it by picking the pup up and starting to tickle her behind the ears. All of her attention however, was not on my dog.

"There's my dad, just parking the car with the trailer. Come and meet him."

The man who emerged was wearing a scout leader uniform. After the introductions, Bernie Baxter was quick to suggest, "Two more helpers, hey?"

I looked at Martin, thinking *Why not?* He'd had no other plans for the day, and I liked old houses.

"Many hands make light work," Baxter continued. I caught Naomi's skyward look.

"Okay," Martin agreed.

"If Lucky-pup won't be in the way," I added.

"Won't be spoilt rotten," Martin said under his breath, as two much younger girls spotted the pup in Naomi's arms.

Baxter drew out some keys from his pocket and headed for the front door. We followed Naomi and half a dozen other scouts.

Inside was a mess. Piles of newspapers, old clothes, empty cans and bottles, and more stuff that was unidentifiable. It might have been the mouldering remains of take away food containers. That was just the front room. The smell was a mixture of mildew, dust and old rotting stuff. Lucky-pup was twisting like a dervish, trying to take it all in. I took her back from Naomi as Baxter gave the scouts directions, starting with basic stuff like "wear your gloves at all times" and "any injuries to be reported immediately". He had brought a supply of gloves, industrial strength rubbish bags and whatever else he thought might be needed.

The long passageway through to the back of the house was blocked where the ceiling had collapsed. Rather than walk over the mess, Baxter said, "Okay, get started bagging rubbish in here. Tom, you're in charge. I'll go round the back and see what it's like from there."

The garage blocked most of the driveway side of the house, and the little gate there was blocked by who knew what on the other side. The other side of the house had a narrow concrete walk way and this led to the back. We had to sidle past two rusty kids' tricycles and an adult bike, and came out beside a rotten wood lean-to shed. Once past that, the riotous growth of grass, weeds and scrubby trees in the back yard became visible. The full effect though, was daunting. Weeds were growing up through piles of junk, mostly metallic and rusting. There was at least one old car, a fridge, two old bed frames, the inside of an old washing machine and an old laundry trough.

Fortunately, the concrete path was relatively clear, except for some pots of dead weeds, a bucket and hose, and a wall mounted clothes line.

The back door, though locked, pulled open easily. The back rooms of the house were no better than the front ones. Laundry, toilet, bathroom, kitchen, and bedrooms – all held more junk, as well as bird and rodent droppings, leaves and twigs, and the walls were water stained.

Lucky-pup wriggled, getting herself free and running off before I could grab her lead. I chased her into the kitchen, but she disappeared into an adjoining room. Trouble was, the space she had vanished into was too small for any human. Her excited yips were muffled.

My impolite curses caused Mr Baxter to look at me. He did call through into the front of the house to "catch the dog if she comes through." I wondered what the idiot pup had found.

We enticed Lucky-pup to return by knocking a bent fork on one of the revolting discarded food tins. It hadn't taken her long to recognise that sound. Since I didn't have anything to give her, I made a fuss of her while Naomi went to fetch some empty boxes from the van outside.

She returned with rubbish bags as well, plus some gloves for Martin, me, and herself.

"We'll start in the kitchen," she told her dad. Then she told us, "Green bag for cans and bottles that can be recycled. Stack papers outside the door, and put rubbish in the black bag. Anything still usable, can go in the boxes. Some of it we might keep, but the rest can go to the op-shop."

I asked, "Do you think all this stuff was here before the owner left?"

"Who knows if the woman who lived here owned it or not. She might have been a squatter. But no. All sorts of people have used this place. Oh! Put some gloves on!"

Lucky-pup lost her comfy resting place and I put the end of her lead around the leg of a metal framed kitchen chair. She went back to sniffing everything within reach. Martin began to bag the most obvious rubbish, going back to his more normal taciturn. Naomi and I went to investigate drawers and cupboards – chatting as we found various oddments. Something caught on my latex glove and it tore.

"Dad has a whole box of them in the car. I'll get more," Naomi volunteered.

I didn't think I needed gloves to pull out saucepans from a low cupboard, but as soon as I touched a huge aluminium pot images began to fill my head. It was as if I was using that very pot to protect myself from someone hitting out with something like a wrench or spanner.

"What's up?" Martin asked, breaking the vision.

"Oh, nothing," I lied. These flashes were coming more often, but not everything I touched gave off emotional visions. "I think my gran had one of these – for preserving stuff. There might be jars around."

"There was. Mostly broken. If I find any intact ones, I'll bring them over."

As a test, I touched some of the pots and pans we had already boxed. More flashbacks, this time of pots being set up above the back door to fall if anyone came in. I wondered at the sad life of the woman who had lived there.

Lucky-pup finally curled up for a sleep, but raised her head each time someone walked through. There had been the building inspector, plus utility company reps checking that the power and gas were off and reading the meters. I found a surprisingly clean saucepan, and put some of my bottled water in it. I took Lucky-pup outside. She took a drink, and emptied about that same amount out near a plant pot, and began sniffing around. She led me to a low door that gave access to under the house.

"No way, dog! I don't know what might be under there. Spiders for a start."

For a critter that was less than two months old, she was determined to try and scratch her way under the door. I picked her up and took her inside.

"The silly creature has a liking for holes," I told my friends.

"Maybe she put herself in that damned drain," Martin said. "And now she assumes she will be rescued from any others."

By lunchtime, when we stopped for a pizza lunch, a lot of the clearing had been done. The older males – scouts, parents and leaders had removed the debris from the collapsed ceiling. We were able to look into the room between the front lounge and the kitchen. All three rooms had once had fireplaces. In the kitchen, that alcove contained an old combination gas stove and electric oven.

The centre room had rubbish in the grate, but it seemed to be where the former resident had slept. At that, it wasn't much. A wire spring bed base supported a thin mattress and threadbare sheets. These had been left rumpled. Next to the bed were boxes – used as tables and for keeping clothes in. A few objects, possibly personal mementoes, still stood on the mantle over the fire place.

"Is the woman who lived here still alive?" I found myself asking.

Baxter had heard the question.

"I believe that she is, but she isn't likely to be returning. The council took possession of the property and offered it to us."

"Should we put personal stuff aside for her?"

"If you want. I will leave that to you."

Baxter left to respond to a call. Naomi asked, "What's with that pup?"

Lucky-pup was staring at the fireplace. I moved closer, but only so the extent of the leash let her sniff but not touch the place. "Hopefully it's only old food remains, not rodents."

When my phone chirped, indicating a message, I removed a glove to reply to my mum's, "What are you up to?" question. The time had flown and it was later than I had expected. Not that it was a problem.

Getting back to packing stuff from the centre room, I reached for a dusty frame, and roughly wiped the dust off. Just touching it with a bare hand brought intense images.

The aged photo showed two little girls with ash blond hair – like enough to be twins. In my mind, I saw them laughing, crying, dirty, in the bath, being fed, getting dressed, and playing with toys or riding trikes. They looked no older than the static kids in the photo. Were they the woman's kids? I dropped the frame in the keeping box, before Naomi noticed my abstraction.

A glance around the room showed no signs that the girls had

been there. Maybe there was child stuff in some of the other rooms. Though, Martin had said the place had been empty for ages – those kids could be grown up by now.

Mr Baxter came in and announced, "That's enough for today. Both the van and the truck are full."

Naomi gave an audible sigh of relief as she straightened up. To her father she said, "These two boxes are personal stuff, and the clothes might be okay for the op-shop – but they will need cleaning."

I dared to ask, "I'd like to clean up the personal stuff and maybe take it to the lady."

The vague frown on Baxter's face suggested to me that he didn't like the idea. "I can try to find where she is, and what her carers think."

*What did he know that he hadn't said?*

I glanced at Naomi as if to ask, "Do you know anything about the woman?" but she shook her head.

When I looked around for Lucky-pup, who I had seen not that long ago asleep on a ripped padded arm chair, she had vanished. *Damn!*

The fork and can trick only yielded faint yapping. It was loudest in the centre room, but still muffled. She wasn't under the bed, and we checked behind all the piled stuff, finally deciding the sound was loudest by the fire place.

Naomi went to check the front room, and I went to the kitchen. No one had seen her. I went outside with the can and tin and tried again. Martin had followed me.

"The yipping is getting louder."

"I bet that girl-dog is under the house!" Martin exclaimed. He turned to go get something to cut the padlock on the door.

Once the door was open, a proud looking Lucky-pup pranced out, half dragging a small child's shoe.

I picked up my dusty, cob-webby brown dog and growled at her. She had somehow slipped her leash as well. When I tried to take the shoe from her mouth, she didn't want to let go, and I had the sudden sensation of suffocating. As soon as I let the shoe go, the feeling went.

"Are you allergic to dust or something?" Naomi asked me.

"Hardly," I said, considering that I was all over dusty from the day's efforts.

"You looked kind of funny for a moment," Naomi admitted.

To cover that, I said, "I was wondering how this mutt got under the house and why the shoe was there."

"There is probably even more junk under there," Martin said. "If anyone has some overalls, I'll go and look."

He didn't give Baxter a chance to object. "It's pretty low under there. I'm not as big as the adults still here, and older than most of the scouts. Besides, I know how girls hate dirty places like that."

One of the fathers said, "I have some overalls in my car."

The scouts and parents still remaining, made a small crowd waiting for Martin to re-emerge. When he did, all he said was, "There is some stuff under there."

When he hadn't brought anything more out, most of the crowd turned to head off home. However, I had seen Martin's face. Okay, it was now very dusty, but under that – his face was white. I went over and let Lucky-pup wriggle over to him. It seemed to snap him out of some kind of shock.

In touching him, during the dog transfer, I had a brief flash and understood his reaction. He had seen bones. Child sized, that Lucky-pup must have begun to unearth.

In Martin's ear, I whispered, "I'll get Mr Baxter to come over." Martin nodded, making a show of patting my dog.

I found Mr Baxter returning from his car, and commented, "I think we need to get a new lock on that door."

I used that as my reason for going to talk to him, but then I said, more quietly, "I think Martin saw something under there."

Baxter's head turned to Martin and he strode over to him.

"What was it?" Naomi asked. I shrugged, but retrieved the shoe that Lucky-pup had finally dropped, and held it with a spare glove.

Naomi studied her father and seemed tense. "Something is wrong," she muttered. "Hang around, Annie."

"Anything I can do, Dad?"

"Yes," he said abruptly. "Tell all the scouts they can head off home. I will be in touch about the next working bee. Tell Ted and Frank to hang around. We will go to the tip later if there is time, but I will have a word with them shortly. How will Annie get home?"

"She came with Martin. Walked. So they can't live too far away."

I heard that and confirmed it. "I have to look for Lucky-pup's lead. She escaped it somewhere. Is it okay if I check inside?"

I received an absent nod from Baxter and a gesture from Martin.

"Take her, will you? I didn't see the lead under the house. Are you right to get home by yourself?"

"Probably, but...let's pretend I am a girl with no head for directions."

Martin gulped. "How did you know?"

I told part of the truth. "Lucky-pup brought out a shoe."

Alone in the woman's bed/living room, I watched Lucky-pup as she returned to sniffing. I was ready to grab the little beast if she looked like she was going to bolt again. I was actually hoping she would go back to where her lead was.

"Do you realise, dog, that we can't go home without your lead?"

She yipped.

*Was that a 'yes' or an 'I don't want to'?*

With one eye on her, I began looking, finally finding one end of the lead caught on a hanging spring at the back of the padded chair. The other end was under it. I moved the chair, and saw that there was an area of the boards that seemed just a little newer than those around. Lucky-pup sniffed one end. I grabbed her and pressed. A pair of boards see-sawed. So that was how she had got under the house.

I dragged the lead out and into my pocket, and the chair back over the hole. Now I had a legitimate reason to hang around.

Most of the people had gone when a plain white car drove up and two men stepped out. I recognised one of them from the other week and the business at school. Martin uttered a low curse.

Martin whispered to me, "You were on the right track with the shoe, but there was other things under there. Syringes and stuff."

He didn't need to say more. Some people still thought the drugs at school were connected to him, and that he had corrupted his cousins.

Baxter had called in the police after Martin had told what he had seen. Now he repeated that to the two detectives. Naomi, standing beside me, uttered a sound of denial, and went pale. I knew how she felt.

"Why did you go under the house anyway?" was the first question Martin was asked.

"To see if there was more junk under there." He was glaring at the men as if daring them to disbelieve him.

I produced the shoe and said, "My dog got under there and brought this out."

"He volunteered," Naomi blurted. "There's not much room under there and Dad wouldn't fit. Most of the scouts here today were the younger ones."

The elder of the two detectives still considered Martin and what he had said.

"And I found out how my dog got under there." That moved all attention to me. "There's something inside that I think you ought to see."

The younger detective went to look in under the house, the other nodded and followed me. Naomi, her dad, and Martin came as well.

"There," I said, pointing out the difference in the wood that had been under the chair.

"You've a good eye on you," the man commented.

"Stuff you pick up being a renovator and architect's brat," I claimed, secretly pleased. "Besides, Lucky-pup was sniffing at it, and her lead was caught on the chair. If you press on one end, the other comes up."

After examining that and shining a torch down, the detectives looked around the room.

"Who was working in here?"

"Annie and me." Naomi indicated our piles – clothes to wash, rags and rubbish, personal stuff and other junk.

"Do you need to look at the stuff," I asked.

"We might want to," the elder detective advised. "Even though it probably won't tell us anything."

"I thought that the personal stuff should go to the lady who used to live here."

That brought a grim smile to the policeman's face. "Old Mad Maude? I doubt that she would even remember the stuff. Besides, she was put away 'at the governor's pleasure' as they used to say."

"What did she do?" Naomi asked, obviously as interested as I was.

I leant against the back of the chair, to put Lucky-pup's lead back on. As the policeman spoke – I saw other images.

I heard, "She was charged with kidnapping babies."

I saw, a happy child on a lap, then men barging in, grabbing the child, grabbing...in this view it felt like me...and hustling me out the door.

I heard, "She lost her own children – no one knows what happened to them. So she went looking for them, took a boy from a pram and a girl from a car."

Naomi looked at me. "That poor woman."

Martin had clamped his mouth shut, but I was sure that everyone was wondering if what he had found were some remains of the woman's missing children.

### Chapter 4

"Where can we find you if we need to?" the elder detective asked.

Naomi's dad handed over a business card, Martin and I gave our addresses. We each received a card from him in return. It reminded me that I should be getting home, before it got dark.

The detective had a final word. "We'll need to seal this place off, and I would appreciate that you didn't discuss what was found with anyone else."

"I should give my folks some idea, in case you come calling," I said. That was allowed.

Sunday morning, I listened to the radio and TV news but heard nothing about our find. It wouldn't stay that way, I predicted. Drugs and bodies in a soon to be scout hall? Too juicy for any slow news day.

I was supposed to be catching up on the homework I'd not done yesterday, but I couldn't concentrate. Instead, I took out an A4 binder book and added some extra entries. This was where I had decided to record the various 'images' I had seen – as well as the context. I had started it two weeks ago, and included the outcomes I knew of.

Now I wrote down all the flashes that I had yesterday – as well as the oddments or items they were attached to.

I wanted to know more about Mad Maude, so I included the snippets I had heard about her.

Even if they had no proof, the police seemed to think she'd killed her own children. Nothing I had 'seen' gave a full story, and I wanted to know the truth – if I could. Particularly if the poor woman was really a victim of someone else.

All I felt I knew was, that she'd once had kids she loved, someone had taken a child from her and taken her away, once she had been attacked, and she had been scared enough to rig makeshift alarms on her door. That left me with so many questions, starting with why she had been sleeping in the family room, not one of the bedrooms. So many years had passed though, and many strangers had made use of the house – I might end up getting mixed images.

The internet was my next thought, and I got so intent that I jumped when Mum called me for lunch. I had jotted down notes from various old newspaper articles about Maude Delaney. They all implied her guilt.

With or without the news media – word had got around. The police tape circling the old house would have been enough to get tongues wagging. I heard odd snippets when I went to the shops with Mum.

Most of the stories going round would have done a fantasy writer proud. None were completely accurate. The wildest tale I heard was that the scouts had found an abandoned meth lab. That was closely followed by the scouts finding a drug cache or a dead junkie. Most people knew that Maude had lived there.

A woman, going through the checkout ahead of us, was telling he checkout operator her view of things. The latter, began to say something once or twice, but managed to refrain from adding her own view.

When our turn came, I casually raised the same subject by shaking my head, and commenting, "I can't see how any sensible person can think that stuff that happened in the past decade was the responsibility of someone who hasn't been there for twelve years."

I made eye contact with the woman and rolled my eyes.

"It's just talk," the woman, whose badge read 'Tina', said. "They didn't know Maude, so they can think that anything is possible."

"It sounds like you did know her," my mum commented.

Tina nodded. "She was an excellent worker, even though the scope of what she could do was limited. She was good doing the routine, repetitive stuff – until her accident."

"What happened?" I asked.

The woman shrugged. "Her husband said she fell and hit her head and that she couldn't work anymore. I went to visit her at home a little while later. She was on her own and it seemed she couldn't even look after herself."

"I heard her children were taken from her," I said. "That's so sad. Didn't she have any family to help her?"

"She was the last of the Hartleys. Her parents had died some years before."

"And why didn't her husband help her and the kids?"

The woman snorted softly. "They weren't his kids. Not that it would have made any difference."

On my way home, I got to thinking. When I told my parents what had been found at the scouts' clean up – Dad had advised staying out of the matter. Though he was interested in the intended restoration of the house.

"There's stuff at the house that is Maude's. I thought it would be nice to take it to her."

My mum frowned before saying, "They may mean nothing to her, or they may upset her."

"How can I find out?"

"Maybe the police can tell you."

"Would she still be in some state-run mental institution?"

"I couldn't say. It depends on the state of her mind. She would not be released if she was still a danger to others."

The visions I had seen of Maude, seemed to be of her as a victim. If the man I had seen was her husband, he was the dangerous one. Perhaps the other private stuff I had put aside would tell me more – if they hadn't been handled too much by others.

Then something occurred to me. "Mum, if Maude was as simple as that woman implied, and unmarried when she had her children, would it be usual to let her look after them by herself?"

"What on earth has you so fascinated, Annie?"

I shrugged. "I feel sorry for her."

Mum sighed. "Probably, when she had them, a council nurse would have visited her for a time. If she was managing well and the babies were doing well, there would be no reason to consider placing the babies in care. By then, they had stopped encouraging or forcing single mothers to put their babies up for adoption."

"Forced?" I queried. I felt a jolt of pity, recalling my vision of a child being dragged from Maude's lap.

"It happened," my Mum admitted. "Why don't you see what the police turn up and report in the papers?"

It seemed that she wanted to change topics. "Did you get any of your homework done?"

"I'll finish it later."

"Tell me about Martin. Your dad was concerned."

"Ow, Mum! I told him Martin was nice. He's a loner at school and some people don't like him but he rescued Lucky-pup. He can't be bad if he did that. And he gave us all that doggy stuff too."

"How's your new friend? Abbie, was it?"

That was an excellent question, and I couldn't really answer it. I side stepped it by saying, "She and I have made it a game to see who completes maths problems fastest."

The real fact was that on Friday, Abbie hadn't been at school at all.

On Monday, Abbie wasn't at homeroom. A little way into the first period, maths, she slipped into the seat beside me, giving me neither a greeting, nor a look.

*Well, if that was how she wanted it...*


We were meant to be doing exercises, but Abbie had missed the class where we learnt to do them. She was only pretending to work by looking in her book. From the side, I could see that her eyes were red and puffy. I wondered if Gill had told her off, or if something else was the matter.

I paused in my work and slipped out a plastic page protector with a copy of my notes for the last lesson. Without being obvious, I slipped them across to Abbie. She realised what they were, and glanced at me. I gave her a tentative smile. A terse, whispered "Thanks" was all I got, but Mr Tucker didn't like chatting in his class, and he was beginning to walk our way.

"Trouble, Ladies?"

"No, Sir. I was just giving Abbie a copy of my notes from the last lesson."

Abbie added. "I was going to read the section in the book, and the notes and try the problems before asking for help."


I had found the topic easy to follow, and expected Abbie would as well. That was unless she had too much other stuff on her mind.

"Can I borrow a pencil sharpener?" I asked in a low voice when Tucker was well away.

She reacted as I had hoped, just pushed her pencil case my way. Considering that she had been hugging all her stuff when she walked in, I wasn't surprised to get flashes of images when I touched the pencil case.

First thing I saw was Gill giving her a thorough dressing down. There was no sound, but the emotion Abbie had felt was intense. She was late without a note. Were they really that tough about that? Or was there more to it in her case? Anyway, she had a lunchtime detention, but oddly, that was more of a relief to her than a cause for anger.

When I finished with the sharpener, and was putting it away, I had another flash.

Two strangers, a man and girl, older than Abbie. He had long dark hair all in tight little plaits, and she was blond, but her hair was frizzed. They stuck their faces in Abbie's, saying something that frightened her. These visions usually went backwards, so I saw then the strangers searching a room with Abbie wanting them to stop.

While trying to do the next problem, my mind was berating me. I should have mentioned the light! But what good would that have done? I knew Abbie was there alone, but she wanted no one else to. She would have lied, and said it was the housekeeper, or a flash from the car headlights. Still, she was here, not obviously hurt in any way.

*What could I do? What would she let me do?*

When the bell went, I asked her, "Are you okay?"

"Of course I am! There's nothing you can do for me, Charity Case."

*Ouch!* Martin was right, but she didn't have to be like that!

"You sound back to normal, that's good." I walked off. I didn't need to have my kind intentions slammed back in my face.

I kept away from Abbie and her friends at the break and after that we had different classes. I made myself concentrate in Italian to put her rudeness out of my mind. You couldn't force someone to accept your help.

Too bad I didn't have anyone to help me with Italian. I could do without extra revision sheets to catch me up. So far I had managed to put off the idea of an extra class after school.

I was quite ready for lunch by the time I'd picked up my extra homework, so I wasn't at all pleased to hear Gail, Helen, Claire and Abbie. They were around the lockers, so I dallied just out of sight, but not out of earshot.

"It's probably slipped between pages in your folder," Helen was saying.

"I've looked in all my folders," Abbie argued. "I need to find it."

"Well, if you don't hurry to detention, Gill is going to be all over you."

"He's just being lousy because of last week."

"When you taught the Charity Case a lesson?" Gail snorted. "That wasn't a punishment he gave you then."

"Probably because of the new girl," Claire decided. "If she got in trouble again, I bet she'll see a different side of him."

"Maybe we should..." Helen began, speaking slowly.

"Don't be stupid," Abbie snapped. "You'll only get in trouble and he will blame me for putting you up to it. Look, I'd better go, can you look around here? In case it dropped out earlier?"

"Sure, Abs," Gail agreed. However, to my delight, they left through the far door as soon as Abbie had gone off.

I hurried to get my lunch, hearing the wind gust through the locker area and blowing some dry leaves around. As I was about to close my locker, I saw the corner of some paper protruding from under the lockers. I pulled it out, and found it was an envelope. Maybe this was what Abbie lost? I didn't have time to check the writing on it, as Karen was calling for me. I just slipped it in my top folder and locked my locker. There was no rush. Abbie was in detention, and anyway, she'd said there was nothing I could do for her! She could wait. And it might not even be her stuff.

It wasn't until I opened my folder to do my Italian homework that I remembered the envelope. Seeing it, I figured that I should check to see if it was Abbie's. The envelope had a return address for the Registry of Births, deaths and marriages. If this was Abbie's birth certificate it would explain her freaking. I didn't know if her birthday was soon or not, but if she was nearly sixteen, she might be wanting to get her learner's permit. I know I was looking forward to learning to drive.

Deciding I had better see if my thought was right, I picked the envelope up. There was no recipient address showing in the envelope's clear panel, so I felt for the folded contents.

As soon as my fingers touched it I knew these pieces of paper had caused some kind of disagreement. Abbie had been very upset by something the strangers had said.

I found the addressee, Jeffrey Carson, but the details on the birth certificate were for a Gabrielle Hartley. My jaw dropped open. Why had Abbie's father ordered a copy of Maude Hartley's daughter's birth certificate? There was no father's name mentioned, had it been him? Did Abbie think this was her? The age could be right. In fact the birth date was just over a week before mine. But no one knew what had happened to Maude's children, and if he had this birth certificate, why not that of the other daughter?

Thursday evening, Naomi and I were working on a history project, at her house, when the doorbell rang. Voices from their lounge room were muffled, and we ignored them as the work was due in a couple of days. However, when there was a knock on the door and her Dad called us, we had to stop.

"What is it, Dad?"

"Someone who would like to talk to you," Baxter said, adding, "Both of you."

We looked at each other, then got up from her desk.

Bernie Baxter, Naomi's dad, gestured to the lounge room, but said, "We will be able to get back to the cleaning up on the weekend."

"That's great, Dad. So the police have finished there?"

Baxter just shrugged for us to follow.

We immediately recognised the younger of the two detectives that had been at the house the previous Saturday. His voice had a touch of an Irish accent, and his face was one used to smiling. He greeted us both, and introduced himself, then Naomi repeated her question to him.

DC Gareth Kelly told us, "We have done all we can do. I doubt that any samples taken for forensic analysis will yield anything useful. The scene is too contaminated."

I found myself asking, "Did you find a child's body under the house?"

Kelly turned to me, eyes intent. Before he could answer, my furry shadow yipped and I said, "Lucky-pup found a child's shoe, and Martin said she had been digging at something."

"Well, yes we did. However, that is not to be spread around. The child was about three years old."

"Was that all you found?" I persisted.

"Apart from discarded needles and some residue of dried marijuana."

Baxter said, "We are to keep our eyes open while we are cleaning and put aside anything that might potentially be relevant."

"Do you mean drug stuff?" Naomi asked.

"That, or anything else relating to Maude Delaney. Papers for instance."

"Have you identified the child?" I asked.

"Not yet. However, in the stuff you collected there was a frame with two samples of baby hair. A DNA comparison has been requested."

"I still think it would be nice for Maude to have her things back," I said. I looked at Kelly to ask, "Would I be allowed?"

Naomi simply shook her head. "Annie, you're unbelievable."

"I'd have to run that by my superiors," Kelly hedged. "We would like to talk to her too, but apparently she has gone off with some cousin and hasn't returned."

"So, she is out of whatever place the court had her confined?" I persisted.

"She has been at a group home for the past two years. It's in Camberwell. We have been trying to trace this alleged cousin."

"That's why DC Kelly came to see me," Baxter admitted. "He wanted to see the land transfer documents and what I recalled of the man I spoke to."

I still had plenty of questions, but I didn't think I should push my luck any further. So I said, "Maybe I should drag my Dad along to the next working bee. He's an architect, and he's renovated a lot of places. He's in charge of the makeover of a housing estate in Dandenong at the moment."

"That might be an interesting idea, Annie. If he's available. We will need to have an expert look at where the ceiling collapsed."

"And find any other odd hiding places," Kelly suggested, seriously.

When Kelly had gone, I decided that the history of the

diverse cultures in Australia had lost its appeal. I was more interested in the history of the house where Maude Delaney had lived. If history is based on evidence derived from the remains of the past, I wondered how the visions I had endured, fitted into that history. If they were not my imagination, they might be insights that weren't even hinted at in the old news reports, and which went against all the current assumptions.

Lucky-pup, who had only settled down again when I gave her a bone shaped dog treat, caught my distraction and began to try jumping on me. "I'm losing the plot," I admitted.

Naomi laughed. "And I know where your mind is. I assume that means you will be helping out again?"

"You bet!"

"And Martin?" I wondered if she was trying to find out if we were officially a pair.

"I will let him know when it will be. He didn't seem to mind helping last weekend."

"You know, he's different when he's not at school."

"Yeah, and I reckon that's because a lot of people there still think he's some kind of criminal that escaped being found out."

"Well, he didn't get suspended, like Tony and Adam, or expelled, like those year 12 boys," Naomi pointed out. Then in a leap of intuition, she asked, "Is that why you are interested in Mad Maude? Because you think she was blamed for things she didn't do?"

I hadn't actually thought of it that way, but maybe she had been. So, since Naomi had brought the subject up, I told her the things I had overheard at the shops and the comments of the checkout woman at the supermarket. Then I mentioned the ideas I had put to Mum and the things she had said. I didn't mention the birth certificate I had seen and copied.

"She still took those two little kids," Naomi reminded me.

"And everyone thinks she killed her own," I retorted. "But in that picture we found, the two little girls looked happy, clean and cared for. Maybe when she had that accident, if it was an accident, the kids were taken from her without her agreement. If it had made her simpleness more pronounced, maybe she couldn't look after them. But I still don't think she would have killed them and hidden their bodies."

That got Naomi thinking, for she sat in silence for a while. "If you get to go and see her, I'll come with you. It's not like scouts don't visit the old, infirm and simple, to bring them a bit of company."

"Thanks."

"What say we try to finish this assignment at lunch tomorrow?"

I took the offer of a drive home, since it was already dark, and introduced Naomi and her Dad to my parents. The men got talking and arranged to meet on Saturday to look at the old house. I decided to go along, since I liked listening to my dad when he was 'working'.

When I was finally able to get to my room to get ready for bed, I tried to ring Martin to let him know what I'd learnt from the policeman's visit. His phone must have been flat for I had the message that the number was unavailable.

Thinking I could tell him in the morning on the way to school, I put my phone on to charge and went to bed.

However, Martin wasn't waiting for me at the usual place next day, nor was he at school.

The Hells' Angels were living up to their name, taking delight in telling me there had been police cars at the Kemple house that morning when the school bus went past his street. They might have been in the street, but I wasn't going to believe any of their claims. I was worried though. If I knew exactly where Martin lived, I would have planned to go there after school. Martin however, hadn't said much about his home life. Mostly all I knew was that his father drank too much. I tried texting him during the day and received nothing back.

Martin was still on my mind the next day when I got dressed to go with Dad. When he asked me if Martin might turn up, I just shrugged.

Mr Baxter was waiting at the house when we got there and I was disappointed that Naomi hadn't come. Still, that meant that I could follow my dad as he was shown through the house, including the now accessible passageway to the bedrooms. Which were all pretty bare. The police had been all over the place for there was traces of grey powder everywhere.

The trap door under the chair had been enlarged, and was now covered by a row of planks laid side by side. I decided that it was well that I had left Lucky-pup with Mum this time.

Later, when my dad was down to making sketches of what could be done to the house, I heard car doors closing outside, and went to look out. I saw DC Kelly carrying a box up to the front door. He was returning the things I had considered personal to Mad Maude.

He put them inside the front door and told me I could clean them up if I still wanted to. A quick glance told me they had all been dusted for prints. I took him through to where my dad was still discussing renovation ideas, and at the same time lifted my Dad's car keys.

If I thought Kelly would tell me anything, I would have tried to find out if Gail's nasty insinuations yesterday had any truth to them. Instead, I took the box of possessions out to the car.

A few ideas began to run around in my head, triggered by the reminder of Maude Hartley. Part of me thought I ought to mention seeing Gabrielle Hartley's birth certificate. The rest of me could predict the nastiness I'd be subjected to if anyone knew I had seen and reported it.

I had copied it at home, and taken the original back to school. With some lucky timing, I had managed to slip it back into Abbie's locker, with no one noticing. She was probably fretting about who had found it and if they would say anything. I wasn't going to reassure her.

Soon after the detective left, my dad emerged saying to Baxter something about having drawings done and getting a costing of the project. He was humming faintly as we drove home – a sure sign that the project was fascinating him. I tried calling and texting Martin on the way back, still getting no answer.

On Sunday afternoon, I decided to take Lucky-pup for a walk. I found myself going the way Martin had taken me the previous weekend. Coming up to the milk bar where the 'Hell's Angels' hung out, I began to have second thoughts about going past it. I recognised Martin's two older cousins, still on suspension from school and no longer leaders. Others emerged from the shop, and I recognised two of the girls.

Lucky-pup was straining ahead, and when I tried to edge to the kerb to cross the street, she still wanted to go straight ahead.

*Oh, well, I can bluff this out.*

"Well, well, if it isn't Jamieson," one of the Logan twins

drawled. "Hey, cuz, your girlfriend is here."

"Who?" I asked innocently. "I don't have a boyfriend."

I heard two girls snickering and turned. "Hello Gail, Claire." I decided not to mention how they were risking trouble being with the twins. I picked up Lucky-pup and moved to enter the shop.

"Hey, Jamieson. Dogs aren't allowed in there," Gail drawled.

"Oh? I just saw you two coming out," I said casually, and brushed past them. Just that touch on Claire's jumper, made me shudder, and I had a quick mental image of Abbie getting into a car with a boy about the age of the Logan brothers.

I breathed easier once I was inside, and reached the bottled water display.

"Annie, what are you doing here?"

Martin's voice made me spin around, and Lucky-pup yipped a welcome and tried to struggle free. It occurred to me that she hadn't done her usual greet everyone outside. Me, I was very glad to see Martin looking like nothing was wrong.

"Have you been hanging out with your cousins?"

"No. I work here, and if they had half a brain between them, they wouldn't be hanging around here."

The opening of the door made the bell there tinkle. Someone else had come into the shop. Martin turned away and pretended we hadn't just been talking. Seeing his dark haired cousin, Gerry, I guessed why.

"Hey, Jamieson. You can do better than my little cuz,"

"Really? You offering are you? Well, I can do better than a stupid lout like you."

"How's that Jamieson?" His voice took on a dangerous edge.

"Well for a start, Gail reckons you're hers. And secondly, Gail and I are minors, and if we get into trouble because of you... you're history."

Gerry's face went blank as he took that in.

"Though I actually thought for a moment that you had found

a better role model than Jordan."

Martin glanced around and I winked.

"Hey, what? What do you mean?"

"Just that you rushed in here to try to hang off every word your cousin said."

Having delivered my subtle insult, I moved quickly to the counter to pay for the water.

Lucky-pup tried to wriggle to lick the shop owner. He didn't tell me "No dogs" but "What a cute dog."

"She has good taste," I said. "I thought she liked everyone, but it seems not."

The shopkeeper glanced briefly at Gerry as he gave me my change.

I decided to wait until morning to tell Martin what I knew, and to ask if he knew where Abbie went and why he had been absent on Friday. The truth, not the third hand rumours.

# Episode 4

# The Truth Behind the Vision
## (Abbie POV)

### Chapter 1

Abbie Carson paused and listened before unlocking the door. Since her parents had gone away, she was always afraid of coming home and finding intruders inside. Admittedly, there was an alarm system. If that went off, surely her parents would ring and tell her.

The large hall with its marble tile floor tended to magnify any sound but she heard nothing and went in. She knew Annie's dad was watching to be sure she was okay.

She wished her Dad was like that.

She turned on the hall light and went through to the kitchen for a drink. The door to her father's office, next to her parents' bedroom, was closed. It had been locked when he'd gone so she'd not be able to go in there. At least today she'd had a decent meal, even if Annie had cooked it. No one had thought it worthwhile to teach her anything so useful. Her parents didn't believe Home Ec. was a proper subject. They had a housekeeper to do the cooking and cleaning. When her father was out to impress clients, he'd order food and servers from one of the big hotels.

Abbie listened again before going up the wooden stairs. The house, as usual, was eerily quiet. The only sound was that of her shoes on the floor. She let her bag drop loudly, and went to change into the lounging suit she liked to sleep in. She hadn't used her bed since her parents had run off and that's what she reckoned they had done. Something at the school that first week had spooked her dad. She didn't want to think that her father had scammed the textiles teacher as Annie had claimed.

Could the new girl really get images off things or was she just making them up? *Nah! No one could do that!*

But then, the things she had written about her after that comedian Gill had made them swap shoes, had been freakishly accurate.

Gail had said some nasty things about the new girl, calling her Charity Case and other things. But Annie was actually quite nice, so Gail wasn't going to find out that she'd accepted Annie's invitation. Gail would call it slumming, and might even drop her and she couldn't allow that. Her father wanted her to be one of the rich set. He gave her a decent allowance, but somehow Gail had most say about how she spent it. There was usually nothing left to save.

Having got all the maths homework out of the way before coming home, Abbie decided not to start anything else and went to get her pillow and quilt from her bed. She settled into her chair, planning to read a while before going to sleep. Spending the night in the chair wasn't as comfortable as in her bed, but it meant that she didn't sleep as deeply.

Abbie woke suddenly, realising that there was a hand over her mouth and someone was stopping her from getting out of the chair.

Her heart was pounding and she was having trouble catching her breath. "Mmm," was all she could get out.

"Don't scream! We aren't here to hurt you, understand."

Abbie nodded. The hand moved, but the one pushing on her chest did not. "Who are you?"

The face in front of her, seen only in the shadows of her torch, looked demonic.

The owner said, "Thea, check the curtains are closed and put the light on."

Abbie was finally able to move, and she got up from the chair.

"Don't try to be smart!"

With the room light on, Abbie could see that the couple were probably only in their twenties. The woman had purple spiked up hair and matching dyed leather vest and leggings, and the man had a silver studded leather jacket over jeans.

"What are you doing here," Abbie found the courage to say. "I have no money."

"What about your dear, darling Daddy?" the woman suggested.

"He's...he's not home yet."

"When do you expect him?" That was the man.

Abbie didn't know what to say.

"Do you know where he keeps his money? I bet he has a stash in case he has to get away fast."

"Who are you?" Abbie demanded.

"Why? Didn't Daddy tell you he'd been married before and ran out on his wife and kids?"

Abbie stared at the woman and shook her head.

"He's a bigamist too. When he left our mother, he emptied their joint accounts, most of which was her inheritance, and our college accounts. We had to move from a house like this to a shitty hovel."

The man went on, "So, we're here to get what is ours."

"What...what are your names?"

"Oh, I'm Robbo and that's Thea. What's your name, Sis?"

"Abbie."

Thea smirked. "Daddy's little darling no doubt. Some advice. Don't mention us. He won't be happy if he knew you'd met us."

"Why?"

"Because, Sis, when he was pretending to be our dutiful parent, he called himself James Mainwrite. Before that, he was Jacob

Hillier and when he was born he was Joey Duffy."

Thea added, "It took us ages to track him down. It was only when we were going through our Mum's stuff that we found some interesting envelopes with all those names on. He was keeping those identities active, so that no one would figure out that he was all of them."

"Why did he run off?" Abbie asked.

"Why do you think?" Thea snorted. "He was cheating people out of money. Charging them a couple of thousand dollars to arrange a sale of their interest in a timeshare development. He'd claim to have a buyer lined up, ready to buy, and string them along until they couldn't try to get their money back through the bank and that was it. He'd say the buyer's finance fell through, or they'd changed their minds – all sorts of reasonable probabilities. He'd also made sure they knew the fee was non-refundable, recorded their agreement as well."

"How did you find that out?"

"Simple. When the cops came to try to find him. That's when we found out he'd taken all our money."

Robbo wasn't smiling. "So, some advice, Sis. While he is being generous, save your money in an account he doesn't know about."

"How would I do that?"

"Geez, you're ignorant," Thea told her. "Go to the bank and ask them to open one. You will need to identify yourself. Do you have your birth certificate?"

Abbie shrugged.

"It's probably in Daddy's study. What about a medicare card, or an ATM card?"

"I have an ATM card," Abbie was relieved to say.

"How old are you?" Thea asked.

"Fifteen."

"Well, you can get your own medicare card. You can download the form, fill it in and take it to a service centre to hand in. You'll need your birth certificate or a passport there."

"I don't have a passport."

"If you do, it's probably locked away. I didn't find a safe though or any money. Where is the bastard anyway?"

"Interstate. On business."

"And he left you alone?"

"No. The housekeeper is usually here but she had a family emergency. She should be back tomorrow."

The last was a lie, but she hoped these two alleged siblings would leave.

"We'll be back then," Robbo promised. "Remember, don't tell him or anyone we were here. And maybe you should tidy up his office. You'd know how obsessive he is."

It was that last comment that convinced her the two strangers weren't lying and it was enough to terrify her. If her Dad knew about those two being there, he'd run off for good.

Abbie listened as the two retreated downstairs, and when she heard the back door shut, she grabbed her torch and went down to make sure all the doors and windows were locked and the alarm was working in night mode.

At her father's office, she paused and tested the handle. The door moved inwards and she felt a breeze from an open window. As she hurried to close it, she nearly tripped over something on the floor. With the curtain fully closed and the light on, she could see that the room had been ransacked.

Abbie found that sleep eluded her until about four in the morning when she crawled onto her bed and snuggled under the quilt. She didn't wake until it was well past the time she should have been at school. She was not in the mood to face her friends anyway. It was her turn to buy lunches and she had no money left. Nor could she ring the school and say she was sick. They'd want to talk to her mum or dad.

Well, so did she. She considered calling them, because she certainly couldn't call the police. Then it occurred to her that this was the perfect time to look for her birth certificate, and she could clean up a bit at the same time. When she was finished, then she'd call and say she'd just discovered the break in. She didn't want her prints everywhere, so she went off to get a pair of the gloves Mrs Hanson used for washing dishes.

She cleared the floor first, tidying the papers sliding out of folders and hoping the order was still correct. The pile went back on the desk where a slightly less dusty place indicated where they had been. She wondered, as she looked about, how those two alleged siblings had got in. She had been particular in turning on the full system when she was out. Opening the window should have set it off.

Around the back of her father's desk, she checked all the drawers. Stationary, printed letterheads for Rosewood House Investments, brochures about sports betting with the promise of a 65% return on your investment over 12 months. There were no filing cabinets so she looked in the partly opened cupboard. One side had built in filing drawers, the other his printer, scanner and spare blank paper. In a cupboard under that was a box marked 'Family' that had papers roughly squashed back in.

It occurred to her that the two intruders must have seen her arrive home and waited in there before deciding to confront her.

Very strict reminders about not touching her father's business stuff, warred with her need to find her birth certificate. As things were, she couldn't make a worse mess. She'd have a quick look, and then try to call her father. If she sounded panicked, maybe he or her mum would come home.

She found her parents passports and birth certificates, his didn't look like a fake. Was it? But if he had fled, why hadn't he taken it?

The answer came to her. He probably had others in other names. But why wasn't there a passport for her? She found bank statements in her father's name with six figure values in them, and her own with its regular transfers in and multiple smaller transfers out. She found a bunch of photos in an envelope – her and her mother at various ages. None of her father, but he was probably taking the photos. There were none of her as a baby, which was odd. Or was there a baby album somewhere? Yes, that must be it.

Finally, she found a loose photo – a baby on a man's lap. It looked like a younger version of her father, so it must be him and her. She slipped that in her pocket.

As she was putting the papers and photos away more carefully, she found a sealed envelope with her name on it. The envelope was from the registry of Births, deaths and marriages – like those with her parents' certificates. This went into her jacket pocket and she decided she needed to leave. The box lid fitted better now, and she replaced the box and shut the cupboard.


Back in her room, Abbie hid the photo and envelope amongst her school notes. Her heart was thumping, so she opened her iPad to play her music. After pacing for a while, she said aloud, "I need to photocopy my birth certificate and then put the original back. If I need an original, I will have the data on the copy."

Then, she considered what her supposed sibs had said. It made sense. So she would have to find out exactly what she would need to be able to get Youth Allowance when she was sixteen. Gail's older sister couldn't get it because her parents earned too much. Claire's brother could, but only because she had all those younger sibs.

Would she be allowed to get a job at McDonald's or somewhere? She didn't think so and didn't know how to apply either. Should she try calling Mrs Hanson again? The housekeeper usually transferred her allowance if her parents were away. She'd not answered her recorded messages either.

A short while after leaving the latest message, her phone rang.

"Abbie, dear! I'm so sorry. I can't get back. My mother needs constant nursing and we are trying to find a place for her."

"Can you at least transfer my allowance?"

"Of course dear, and I will transfer some extra for groceries. You poor dear. What have you been eating?"

"Tin stuff, that just needs heating. Really, I've been okay. I am fifteen you know."

"Of course you are, dear. When are your folks due back?"

"On the weekend, I think. But it's okay. Mostly I'm at school and I keep the door and window alarms on."

"You're a good girl, Abbie. I'll transfer the money tonight."

Abbie sighed with relief. At least she could pacify Gail to a point. But she would claim to only have $40 in her account. The others would just have to have a cheap lunch.


Her intention to photocopy her birth certificate before homeroom had to be postponed because the school bus was running late. Then, Gill spotted her and called her into his office.

"Do you have a note to explain your absence on Friday?"

"Um, no, Sir."

"So, why were you? We received no call in, either."

"Sir, my folks had to go off unexpectedly. Mrs Hanson wasn't able to come in until the afternoon. I'd been throwing up during the night and went back to bed."

"And the note?"

"I did ask Dad to write it, but I guess he forgot."

"You will need to bring one tomorrow or you will have another lunchtime detention. I will give you a slip for your homeroom teacher." Gill wrote quickly. "Off you go. You will report to the library annex at lunchtime."

Abbie scowled as she strode away. Maybe she could get Gail to forge her mum's writing? She'd done it before for Helen.

Just then, she needed to hurry. She'd missed homeroom, but needed to catch Mrs Sutton and pass on the note as well as dump her bag and get her maths stuff. Tucker didn't like late arrivals to his class. Damn Gill anyway.

The classroom door was partly open and there was an empty seat just inside, next to Annie. She slipped into it and checked the board for the work. Damn, it was something new.

Tucker was approaching as she tried to look ready. She didn't need him annoyed with her as well. Then she saw what Annie slid across to her. Worked examples! "Thanks!"

As she opened her folder, she heard, "Trouble, ladies?"

Abbie tried to think what to say to the teacher, but Annie was ready to explain.

"I made Abbie a copy of my notes to read."

That gave her the idea to add, "I was going to read the section of the book, and the notes and try the problems before I asked for help."

That worked, getting his words back in his face, Abbie decided. Tucker didn't comment on her late arrival.

"Can I borrow your pencil sharpener?"

Abbie, watching the teacher still, had her mind on what she needed to do just shoved her pencil case towards Annie. She didn't want attention from Tucker.

Abbie kept her mind busy, catching up on the problems and getting the idea of the topic. The bell almost made her jump.

She heard Annie ask, "Are you okay?"

Still trying to forget her fright on Thursday night, and the revelations she couldn't quite disbelieve, she didn't think to modify her tone.

"Of course I am. There's nothing you can do for me, Charity Case."

Annie stood, grabbed her stuff and said, "You sound back to normal. That's good."

Abbie watched her walk off. She didn't need little Miss Goody sticking around. Or freakishly learning her secrets.

Textiles was a slacker lesson than Maths, and Abbie was enjoying designing a dress for herself and was intent on learning how to create a pattern from her sketch. Gail's design was fancier, but would be a lot fiddlier to get it right. Helen was designing a riding outfit and Claire a cheer leader like outfit. They still had time to hiss at her, "Where were you on Friday?

We had to go without lunch."

"I was sick, okay?" Abbie retorted.

"You're paying today," Gail whispered.

"Yeah, okay. But I only have $40 left in my account. Dad forgot to transfer my allowance."

"It'll cost you double next time."

Abbie shrugged. "You'll have to hurry though. I've got detention at lunch."

"Alright, tomorrow. Claire can pay today."

They left her alone then, but Abbie decided that Gail might indeed agree to forge a note for her if it meant she didn't get another detention the next day.

As she hurried to the lockers, Abbie gave herself a moment to smile. Gail had indeed written the note, copying her mother's flowery writing style. Her friend was getting bossier, and that was becoming annoying, so any victory over her was to be enjoyed.

Her amusement evaporated when she rifled through her folder to find the envelope with the birth certificate. She was going to copy it at the library after detention.

"Damn! Where is it?" She swapped back to the folder she'd returned with and checked there.

"What are you looking for?" Helen asked, arriving behind her.

"Something I need to photocopy."

"It probably slipped between pages," Helen offered.

"I've looked in all my folders," Abbie argued. "I need to find it?"

"Well, if you don't hurry to detention, Gill is going to be all over you."

"He's just being lousy because of last week."

"When you taught the charity case a lesson?" Gail snorted. "That wasn't a punishment he gave you then."

"Probably because of the new girl," Claire decided. "If she got in trouble again, I bet she'll see a different side of him."

"Maybe we should…" Helen began, speaking slowly.

"Don't be stupid," Abbie snapped. "You'll only get in trouble and he will blame me for putting you up to it. Look, I'd better go, can you look around here? In case it dropped out earlier?"

"Sure, Abs," Gail agreed, and she did an idle look around.

Abbie hurried off, her mind in turmoil. What if she couldn't find it? Worse, what will Dad do if he finds its missing? He'll find a way to blame me – odds on.

All through detention, she worried about where she could have lost it. She could hope that someone would find it and hand it in or give it to her. Could she have dropped it that morning when she was packing her bag? What if she had, and her parents came home and saw it? Could she hope they would call her when they were on the way home?

No! She had put it in her folder just before putting it in her bag. But the boys had been shoving each other at the lockers that morning and she'd copped some too.

As soon as she was released, she hurried back to her locker to have a thorough look through it, but it wasn't there. The best she could hope that it was found and handed in, not just tossed in a bin. Still, she could still investigate getting youth allowance, and check what her unwelcome visitors had said about a medicare card. There must be a way to get another copy of her birth certificate.

Maybe she should mention it at the office? The sudden shiver she felt made her decide that was not a good idea. If her father couldn't find it – she would act ignorant and blame the intruder.

Yes, maybe it was time to call her parents about the intruder. Maybe that would be important enough to get them to come back – if she wasn't. *When should she do it?*

It would be such a relief to have them back, but if her dad was going to be mad at her, she needed to be able to sound innocent and not be tricked into blurting out the truth.

Friday then. Maybe she'd text them that she was studying with the charity case again. Then got home and went straight to bed – noting nothing wrong until the following day. They wouldn't know it had actually happened a week earlier.

"We didn't find it," Gail said off-handedly. "Maybe it fell out and got kicked under the lockers?"

While there wasn't a crowd, Abbie swiped her ruler around under the lockers. She soon had to stop to get her books. When Annie approached, she hurried to get out of the way, not wanting her to divine what had been worrying her. It was no business of the charity case.

It wasn't until Thursday that Abbie found the envelope in her locker. She breathed a sigh of relief until she realised that the envelope had been opened. It hadn't been ripped, but the gum was unstuck. Hard on that realisation was the question of who had found it and how it had got back in her locker. If it had been handed in and given to Mrs Sutton, she would have just given it to her, and she wouldn't have given her spare locker key to anyone. Her mind flicked to when drugs had been found in Kemple's locker, he'd protested that someone else had done it.

Her skin started to feel like ants were crawling over her. Who had put it there? It had definitely not been there on Monday.

Abbie checked her watch. She should just have time to photocopy it at the library before going to the bus.

The copier was free, Abbie took the sheet out and put it face down and used her student card to activate the machine. She had time to read her father's name and their address on the back before the copy emerged. Then, with only a glance at the copy, it and the original were quickly slipped into her folder, and she ran for the bus.

It was only when she was half way home that she realised that the name on the copy hadn't been hers.

The first thing Abbie did when getting home was to make sure her parents hadn't returned. She had to get the envelope and the certificate back into her Dad's office and the box marked 'Family'. First though, she checked the original – like the copy, the name there was Gabrielle Hartley.

"Who the hell is that?" Abbey muttered. The envelope definitely had her name on it in her father's writing. Had he received the wrong certificate? Given the wrong data? She certainly couldn't ask him, but now she still had to get the right one.

Emerging from the office room, Abbie pulled the door shut. The mystery had to remain her secret, but at least the certificate was back and she could let her father discover the problem. Now though, if she was going to call them about the break in, she needed to create her alibi.

She texted her mother, and said she would be studying with Annie again that evening and having tea there. As she expected, she received no answer. But that was to the good. They hadn't forbidden her to go out. In the morning, she would report the break in.


Abbie woke early and had a quick breakfast and made sure her school bag was ready for her to just grab it and run for the bus. Then, at what was her usual time to get up, she began texting her mother.

"Mum, I really need to talk to you."

After five minutes with no reply she sent, "Mum, I think someone broke into the house yesterday."

Two minutes later, which was probably time for her mother to tell her father and get told what to do – her phone rang.

"Mum!" Abbie's relief wasn't all feigned. She wailed, "What

am I meant to do?"

She heard, "Tell me what you noticed."

As she spoke, she guessed her mother had her on speaker, she heard her father in the background. "The window was forced up, but I closed it. Files from the desk were on the floor. I picked them up. I don't know what else was touched."

"When did you discover this?"

"This morning. I saw the office door ajar, when I knew it was locked when you left."

"Where is Mrs Hanson?"

"Mum, I told you. She hasn't been here. I've been alone."

"Why didn't you see it last night?"

"I sent you a text. I was studying with Annie and went straight to bed when I got home. I had the alarm on."

"Okay, your Father says to make absolutely sure you have the alarm on, and all the windows and doors are locked. Have you had anyone coming to the door?"

"Not after school or when I have been home on the weekend."

"We'll be heading home, sweetheart, but we will be late and we will let ourselves in."

"I'll be so much happier when you get here," Abbie told her.

Abbie looked at her phone when she rang off. The number that called her was unfamiliar, yet she had texted using her mother's number. Odd! Still, it didn't matter. They were coming home. She got her bag, set the alarm, and raced out to catch the bus. It was the only part of her usual routine she had control over.


When she heard the front door open and shut, Abbie raced downstairs and into her mother, hugging her as hard as she could.

"Abigail, please. Let me breathe."

"Sorry. I'm just so glad you're back."

Her father hadn't brought their cases in yet, his first concern was his office. He went there and looked around carefully.

When he emerged he said, "If you had done as you were told and come straight home, they probably wouldn't have broken in."

"You don't know that, Dad. They still might have, and hurt me. And they didn't set the alarm off."

"You can't have set it properly," Jeremy Carson retorted. "Or did you invite that no good boyfriend of yours around? He was only sponging on you, you know."

"I haven't seen him since school went back. He got suspended when it should have been that smelly Martin Kemple."

"Abigail!" Victoria Carson warned. "I can see you have been distraught. Why don't you go and make us all a cup of hot chocolate?"

"There's no milk!" Abbie said reproachfully. "I've had no money to get any and no one to get it for me."

"I will have to have words with Mrs Hanson," Carson said.

"She didn't know. She left a message about a family emergency before you rang here about going away."

"Abigail, enough! I have a lot to check tonight. And I would like you to give me your phone."

"Why?"

"Just get it for me," Carson insisted. A muscle in his cheek was beginning to twitch and his face was reddening.

Abbie took it from her pocket and handed it over. "When can I have it back?"

"When I have a new sim card for it. I don't want those boys from school calling you."

"I have my homework reminders on it," Abbie tried, hoping to get it back. "I will need to check it sometime."

"Don't they have all that on the school website? The school is meant to be the most progressive in the area."

"I keep the password on the phone, I don't remember it."

"If I have time, I will get onto it in the morning," Carson said. "I think you should go to bed now."

Abbie decided it was the best place to be and gave a grumpy, "Good night."

She had no plans to go right to bed, but she got ready in case her mother came to check on her. Instead, she stood near her partly opened door and listened. She heard her father tell her mother to check the message machine. That was something Abbie never bothered to do, except on that first day when her parents weren't around when she got back from school.

There were some messages, and her Mum mentioned them to her father, and took details. Some callers had left no messages. Probably the annoying ones about changing your electricity or gas company. Then there was one, the tone of which gave her shivers.

"Where the hell are you, Carson. I wanna talk to you."

That was all she heard before her father said, "Turn the damn volume down."

Abbie heard no more of that message, or that might have been all of it. She tried to decide if it was the voice of her unmentioned male sibling – but decided he wouldn't ring and give his scarpered father time to repeat his previous behaviour.

Whoever it had been, her parents were now having a low intense conversation. Abbie wondered what was wrong.

Victoria Carson, dressed as she usually did to impress her husband's clients, looked completely out of place in the supermarket. Nor, Abbie decided, did she have a clue about what they needed. At least she herself did, to some degree and she took over pushing the trolley so she could look at each aisle in turn, not criss-cross the store every time something occurred to her mother.

Not that Abbie was concerned about how long the outing took. It was like a dose of freedom after having to stay in the house before and after school and all weekends. After being so confined, she wanted to be able to go to Gail's place or Helen's, but her father had refused. He hadn't even given her permission to go and pick up her favourite magazines from the milk bar. There must be several there waiting for her by now, and her friends were already saying she was a snob and thought herself too good for them.

When they left the supermarket with more than just the stuff they'd need for breakfasts and lunches, Abbie grinned. Her mother hadn't commented, likely hadn't seen, some of the things she'd added. Stuff that health conscious Mrs Hanson would never buy for her. The chocolate would vanish before the bags were unpacked, and her mother considered make-up a necessity.

Neither of them had any idea about what would be needed for evening meals, but they hadn't had to. Jeremy Carson had said they'd order meals from one of the top hotels – not some greasy takeaway food – until he sorted out a new housekeeper.

About that, Abbie thought he was being totally unfair, but he'd never listen to her. All she wanted of him right then was for him to do whatever he intended with her phone so she could have it back. She felt naked without it. Still she dare not push the issue, because then her father might recall she could make calls from her iPad. Then he might want to see it, and she didn't have it. Gail had borrowed it when she had smashed her own. That had been months ago. Maybe her father didn't know what iPads could do.

When she really wanted to growl, "Can I have my phone back?" she asked off-handedly if he had changed the card yet. He snapped at her, "No! I have had more important things to do. My business may be compromised, just when it was taking off. I have to waste time interviewing for a housekeeper, and sorting all the client data."

"Why don't you report the break in?" Abbie blurted without thinking.

"I very much doubt that the police will find the culprits. The people must have been professionals, and I don't want the police nosing in my business. It is too sensitive."

"Abigail, dear, why don't you go and work on your homework in your room?" Victoria Carson suggested. "I know you want to help, but you know nothing about business."

Helping was the last thing she wanted to do, but she didn't say so.

"Could I at least go for a bike ride? I've been cooped up in here for two weeks."

"NO!" Jeremy Carson stated immediately.

Abbie knew not to argue further.

As Saturday proceeded, Abbie felt the need to get out grow more imperative. That morning, she had thought she'd glimpsed her step-sibs and she wondered when they planned to confront her father. She didn't want to be around if they did. Every time the front door bell chimed, she peeked down from her bedroom window, half expecting to see them, but so far, each time it had just been another hopeful applicant.

In a fit of activity, she stuffed a moderately sized back pack with a change of clothes – some that her mother called hoydenish. She added other necessities as well. The idea of sneaking off was growing, but she had no idea where to go yet.

Being in a room with her father was like walking on eggs and trying not to break any. Abbie found him staring at her during their meal that had been sent from the Steak House Grill. He had already made it plain that he believed that the break in was her fault. But it wasn't. The thing was, he had to know that too, so why was he blaming her?

Had the break in got him worried that his latest scam had been figured out. Probably. She was still having trouble thinking that her father might be a criminal, or that the police might come and arrest him. What would happen to her and her Mum if they did?

Was insisting that she not go out a precaution against her saying the wrong thing to someone? And why had the insane idea of him thinking of her as a commodity, and him wondering if it was the right time to sell it, come to mind?

"Can you pass the gravy, please?" Abbie asked as a reason to stare back at her father. He gestured to his wife and concentrated on his food. After a while, when the silence had remained unbroken, she risked a comment. "Helen and Gail are talking about getting their learner's. I was thinking about doing the practice tests on the Vicroads site so I can do the same when I turn 16."

"That's still a good six months off, dear," her mother pointed out.

"I know, but it will take a while to learn all the stuff. And I think I will need a copy of my birth certificate."

She didn't look directly at her parents when she said that, but saw her father stop eating.

"All that can be organised nearer the time," Carson said,

dismissing the issue.

Finally, he finished eating and pushed his plate away. "I have hired a new housekeeper," he announced. "She will be starting tomorrow and living in. I think that will be a much better arrangement."

"Yay!" Abbie said softly, and she caught a faint easing of her father's expression. *Had he expected opposition?*

"Your mother and I will be more at ease knowing someone will be around when we need to be away on business. When we are, we will expect you to heed her. Is that understood?"

"Yes, Dad." Abbie was indeed feeling relieved at his arrangement, even while still resenting the ousting of Mrs Hanson.

During the desert, that her mother had only to bring in from the kitchen, Abbie decided that her father was more relaxed. She hoped he might let her go out the next day.

On Sunday, Abbie broached the idea of her going out to her mother.

"Oh, no, I don't think so. Mrs Buttrose will be coming at eleven and we will need to help her settle in and show her where everything is."

"She might have to get more groceries if she is also going to cook for us. I could help with that," Abbie offered.

"We'll see," her mother temporised. "Your father and I expect you to be helpful and make a good impression on her."

"Will she teach me to cook?"

"Oh, you won't need to cook, darling. "

"What if I decide to get my own place when I'm older?"

"By then, you will be married to a good man, who will be able to take care of you."

Abbie didn't know what to say. Did her father have a potential husband in mind for her already? How barbaric!

Abbie was considering her father's response to her mention of needing a birth certificate, when her mother called her to go downstairs. He'd neither said he had one, nor that he would need to get one. She put that idea aside for later, realising that the new housekeeper had arrived. She smiled and trotted downstairs. It was only when she had her first look at the woman that she realised that she'd been assuming the new woman would be like Mrs Hanson – homely, friendly, middle-aged and dressed comfortably unless important guests were expected.

This Mrs Buttrose was dressed like a fashion model, as if wishing to emulate the lady of the house. The styles were modern, but the fabric was nowhere near as expensive as that of her mother's clothes. Her smile too, seemed more forced than Mrs Hanson's, but that might just be first day nerves. Wanting to make a good first impression, Abbie smiled during her introduction, and offered, "I can show you around."

"There are a few formalities to see to first, Abbie," her father said. "You might get back to your homework for the time being."

He was already gesturing the newcomer towards the formal lounge, so she shrugged and said, "Okay."

She began to head to the stairs, then doubled back to the kitchen. She could hear her father speaking from there, and if she stayed very still make out some of the words. In the mean while she fetched a drink to explain being there.

Her father spent very little time outlining the woman's duties before getting to the topic of his daughter. Abbie's mouth dropped open and she felt herself growing angry – but she knew not to rush in and protest. When she heard Mrs Buttrose ask, "Is your daughter aware of this?"

Her father's answer sent her trotting quietly to her room.

"Abbie is still a child, and a foolish girl at that. I will not risk her running off with unsuitable boyfriends, only wanting her for her inheritance."

Abbie closed and locked her bedroom door and paced the room. Her first furious thought was, *I'm not a child!* Closely followed by, *unsuitable boyfriends*! He's blaming me for meeting them when it was Gail's doing. And he wants me to be in Gail's clique. And now he's using that as a reason to have the live-in housekeeper, jailor more likely, drop her off and pick her up from school. She'd not even be able to hang out with her friends. He was using that business at school as a reason to keep her prisoner.

At least he hadn't suggested making her change schools. She'd be no better than that charity case, Annie, who had been to a dozen schools.

It seemed her mother already knew these plans since she had mentioned why she didn't need to learn to cook. But what in hell did he mean by her 'inheritance'? It sounded like something he expected to happen soon.

She couldn't see either of her parents dying soon, and who else would leave her money? She had never heard either of her parents mentioning parents, siblings or any other relatives at all. Now she wished she had written down the information from both their birth certificates. Then she had a thought that had her stumbling towards her chair.

"Who am I? Am I really this Gabrielle Hartley? And what if I get this inheritance? Will I be allowed to control it?"

The stark answer was, no. While she was still officially a minor, her father would. And then what would happen if he decided he had to run out on everyone?

The voice of Robbo, her alleged sibling, returned to her. "He even cleared out our college accounts..."

Her stomach clenched as if it wanted to eject her breakfast.

There was a knock on her door, and someone tried to open it. Abbie went to unlock it.

Her mother came in. "Abbie dear, come and help Mrs Buttrose."

"Mum, am I adopted?"

Victoria Carson's mouth dropped open. "Whatever made you think that?"

"Am I?" Abbie insisted.

"No. Your father is your father."

"And you? Did you give birth to me?"

Caught without her husband's back up, she didn't know what to say.

"You didn't! So who is my birth mother?"

"Abbie, darling, I am your mother in every way that matters. And you will always be my darling little girl."

"Mum, I'm fifteen!"

"Can we sit down?"

Thinking that she didn't want her father having any chance to overhear, she nodded and closed her door.

Victoria sat in the spare chair, and Abbie used her favourite one. "Let me explain. I couldn't have children. When he bought you home, you were the answer to my deepest wish. You were only about three or four. He said you were the child of an ex-girlfriend of his, who had dumped you with the authorities and given them his name. He didn't need to adopt you. You were his child."

"What's my real name?"

"Why it's Abbie. We had your surname changed to Carson."

"But what was it?"

"Your father never told me."

"Then what is this about an inheritance?"

"You really shouldn't listen in on private conversations, my dear. Anyway, that won't be for a long time yet. The money is tied up and will be for a long time. Now, not a word about that to your father."

Abbie told herself, *No Way!*

Abbie had to put the concerns away to think on later. First she needed to get to know the housekeeper. Mrs Buttrose quizzed her about her daily routine, and Abbie answered as if she hadn't heard that the woman was to drive her the ridiculously short distance to the school bus stop and pick her up there. She was requested to advise her of any outside school hour commitments. She merely nodded and kept quiet about her usual trip to the milkbar to pick up her magazine. However, the woman even knew about that. Had her father been reading her phone messages?

By mid-afternoon, Abbie's pretence of friendly helpfulness had worn thin. She desperately wanted to get out and see her friends. She gathered the backpack she'd put things in earlier and worked on leaving the house unseen.

Abbie grinned when she arrived at the milkbar and saw Gail and Claire there.

"Didn't expect to see you here. You've been snubbing us lately," Gail told her.

"Not my fault. I wasn't allowed to come. Anyway, how come you are still here when Gerry's bike is here. We aren't..."

"Shut up! Gerry didn't do anything. Kemple set him up! You picking up your mags? There's about three of them."

"Want to. But I have a favour to ask. Can I come and stay with you for a day or two?"

"What for?" Gail retorted. "I don't want your father tearing down our door."

"I just want a break from him. He's been like a jailor," Abbie pouted.

"No way!" Gail persisted. "My folks wanted me to separate from all my friends."

"Oh!" Abbie hadn't considered how her friend's parents had reacted. But her own case was worse.

Claire interrupted, "And we've got no spare beds."

"Well, can I borrow your phone to make a call?" Abbie tried.

"Who to?" Claire asked suspiciously. "Anyway, where's your phone?"

"My Dad has it."

"What did you do, Abs?" Gail asked.

"Nothing. He just wants to put a new sim card in it."

"Seems like he doesn't want you talking to us either," Claire pointed out. "Who do you want to call?"

"Adam," Abbie admitted.

"Use the one in the shop," Gail advised. "We'll be in trouble if there's proof we spoke to them. They can get records of mobile calls."

Feeling that her friends were shutting her out, Abbie shrugged. "You're probably right."

"I'm always right," Gail said.

The first person Abbie saw in the shop was Martin Kemple. He might be better than the shop owner for her need. "Do you have change for the phone?"

"Your folks take yours did they?"

She thought he'd not help her, but in the end she caught the coins he tossed her. He turned away and she went to the shop's public phone.

Abbie was relieved when Adam didn't just hang up on her, and elated when he said he'd get his brother to drive him around to pick her up. She ignored Martin, where he was stacking shelves, and went out to wait with her friends.

When the car belonging to Adam's brother drew up and stopped, Adam got out of the car's front passenger seat to open the back door for her. Abbie waved to Gail and Claire when as she got in. Her smile was malicious as she thought, I'll show father that he can't make me a prisoner.

She was surprised how shabby Adam's place really was, but to her it was a palace. Adam took her to his room and put on some music. They both enjoyed the same musicians and bands. They got talking, and Abbie felt herself relax.

Tory, Adam's brother left them alone until coming in and offering to get them all pizza for tea. Finally Abbie got around to asking, "Where are your folks?"

Tory answered, "The Dad's in hospital. Had a heart attack. The Mum's spending all her time there. She'll be back late."

"Oh, I hope your Dad gets better," Abbie said, knowing it was the polite thing to say.

"Mum said he'll have to eat better from now on, but he won't," Adam said.

"I was going to check with your Mum about staying here," Abbie said.

"Won't be a problem," Tory told her. "We'll just say your folks left you alone at home."

Abbie felt a shiver run through her. Could he have known that had been the truth?

"Yeah, Abs, I can fix a bed on the couch for you," Adam volunteered. "It's more comfy than the pull out bed."

It wasn't quite what Abbie thought or expected, and a trickle of alarm filled her. She was alone with two boys, and Tory had been eyeing her during tea. Still, where else could she go? She didn't want to go home.

The strange house had odd sounds, odd smells and the couch was hard. The borrowed pillow smelt of mildew and was almost flat. Abbie couldn't sleep, even when she turned towards the back of the couch and cocooned herself in blankets.

She must have eventually dozed off, for she woke with a hand on her mouth. Memories of a week old assailed her, but this hand wasn't that of her step-sib, but from the cologne smell, belonged to Tory. He had managed to come behind her on the couch and bring one arm around her head. She was held by his body. Her legs were pinioned by his and his free hand was working its way in under the blankets with deliberate intensity.

"Don't know what the kid sees in a skinny bitch like you," Tory whispered in her ear. "But I can show you what a real man can do for a lady."

The blankets stopped her from struggling free when his hand found first her breasts and then moved down towards her pants. Her smothered attempts to call for Adam went unheard, but then a light went on.

"Tory Michaelson! What are you doing?"

The feminine voice was loud and irritated. "You know I said none of your floozies were to come here."

Tory rolled to the floor after withdrawing his hands.

"Ah, Mum. It's nothing. Just trying- "

"I know what you were trying you daft fool. Do you realise how young she is?"

Abbie had rolled over and was keeping herself covered.

Tory scrabbled to his feet. "I wasn't doing anything."

"You were," Abbie said.

"Get out of my sight. Now! Or I will ring the cops and ask them if it were nothing."

Tory didn't quite trot from the room.

"Now, who are you?" That demand was directed at Abbie.

"I'm Abbie, Mrs Michaelson. I asked Adam if I could spend a night or two here. Just until my folks got back." It was only partly a lie.

"Did you think about getting my boy in more trouble? Or are you too dumb to realise what that restraining order business means?"

"Mrs Michaelson, I know Adam didn't do anything wrong," Abbie said, hoping to improve her position.

"You're damned right he didn't. But you rich girls are still trouble. They come here looking for you and my boy's going to have to go to court. You too, you dumb fool."

"I'll leave tomorrow. First thing." Abbie meant it too. She was embarrassed, humiliated, and feeling dirty. Not to mention aware of how far Tory might have gone.

"Too right, and you don't mention being near my lads. They're good boys when girls like you don't tempt them."

Abbie drew the blankets higher around her, to hide how fiercely she was blushing. She heard Adam's mother move away, but nothing else as blood was pounding in her ears.

Sometime later, she was woken by loud knocking on the door. It was repeated with greater intensity. Then, Mrs Michaelson called out, "I'm coming, damn you. Can't a woman get any sleep anymore?"

Abbie heard her say, "Now what is it you want?" The reply was soft, and she moved the blanket to try to hear.

"Who? Oh, her! Yes, she's here. Said her folks were away. Told her to take a hike first thing in the morning. Don't want the stupid little bitch getting my lads in trouble."

Abbie cringed and wished the couch would swallow her. How had the police known to come there? She sensed a presence nearby and tried to feign sleep.

"I know you are awake, Miss Carson. You are going to have to come with us."

"I don't want to go home. I hate my father."

"Unfortunately, Miss Carson, you cannot stay here. You will come with us to the station and we will call your parents."

"I don't want to go," Abbie insisted.

The hands grabbed her firmly and began to pull her upright. She had no choice and she knew it. Now her father really would kill her.

"Anyway, they aren't really my parents. I'm just someone my father got lumbered with because some old girlfriend didn't want me and said he was the father because he's rich."

"We will sort all that out at the station," the policewoman insisted.

Abbie rolled to look at her and decided she looked capable of dealing with people twice her size.

"Alright, but I still don't want to go home."

"We could, if you insist, keep you in a cell overnight. No? Then get up, get dressed properly, get your things and come."

Cornered, Abbie reached for her outer clothes, and stood up. The woman stopped her. "You have blood on your pants."

Abbie immediately thought, *My period isn't due yet.*

"Bring your clothes to the bathroom."

In that privacy, with the constable questioning her, Abbie finally admitted what happened.

"Do you want to press charges?"

Guessing what that would mean, she shook her head. "I shouldn't have come"

"To late for that now. You are just lucky that he didn't go further. We will get a doctor to look at you."

"Do you have to?"

"It is for your protection. We will want a statement, even if you won't press charges."

Abbie heard another official voice saying, "I need you and your two boys to come to the station in the morning. There is the matter of breaking the restraining order and maybe other charges."

Tory and Adam had emerged. The former said, "You don't need me there, I didn't have to keep away from the little tramp."

"Still, we would like a statement from you as to why you came and picked her up."

That was all Abbie heard clearly, for she was hustled out and could only guess that Adam's mother was giving the officer a piece of her mind. The police woman wasn't taking any chances, for she maintained her arm grip, and after directing Abbie into the back seat, took the seat beside her.

When the other officer emerged, he went to the driver's seat, started the car and just before moving off reported via radio, that they were returning to the station with 'the girl'.

The next few hours were a nightmare. More questions,

making a statement, being examined by a doctor with her father hovering just out of sight, and insisting on knowing everything. His presence had kept Abbie from saying much about her reasons for leaving home. Including having been left on her own for two weeks. Finally, she was charged over disregarding the order to keep away from Adam and the other boys involved with drugs from her school, told when to be in court the following morning, and all the time aware that her father's posture was rigid with more than just anger.

Once she was allowed to leave, Jeremy Carson grabbed Abbie's arm and pulled her out to the car. All the way home, he said nothing, but once inside his house, with the door closed he exploded.

"You little slut. I would like to beat you senseless right now. Not only have you embarrassed me by having to go to the police station to get you, you have to go to court and have your stupidity aired in public. You are no better than your mother."

Deliberately reacting. Abbie yelled, "My mother isn't stupid!"

Carson was so angry that he said, "Victoria isn't you mother. You are the child of some slut who was trying to spite me."

Abbie hadn't expected him to blurt it out, but now she knew what her mother had said was true. "Who am I then?"

"I just told you. And right now you are an ungrateful bitch who will be lucky not to get sent to jail after this. And if you manage to wriggle out of that, you had better not step out of line again or I will have you sent to a convent boarding school."

That threat silenced Abbie and once again she wished she could sink into the floor.

"You won't be able to fornicate with boys there! Now get out of my sight before I lose control and beat you senseless."

Abbie was only too happy to get away from her father, but as she ran up the stairs, she saw a shape following her. It wasn't her mother, but the new housekeeper, her jailor.

Yet the woman wasn't smiling, but did speak calmly. "You

will sleep better if you have a shower first to relax you. I will just turn your bed down for you."

After being in the shower twenty minutes, trying to scrub away the memory of Tory Michaelson's hands touching her, she emerged to find a hot drink beside her bed. Her bed was warm too, so the house keeper had turned the electric blanket on too. She was grateful for both, even though the chocolate tasted odd. Once in bed, she had little time to worry about the morning.

# Episode 5

# Not a Chip from the Block

## (Martin's POV)

### Chapter 1

Martin Kemple was not in a hurry to get home. He never was. Arriving after his father had crawled home and passed out was a better option. Though, for some reason, the old sot hadn't been so drunk the past two nights. The night before, he'd been downright nervy, and the night before that - angry about something. Martin had quickly sought his room and locked the door. He didn't want to know what illegal deal had gone sour on him.

While he slouched his way back home, he let his mind think of Annie Jamieson. Then he remembered the tiny bones her crazy mutt had begun to unearth. That poor little kid, hadn't even had a chance to have a rotten life, let alone a good one. To banish such thoughts, he brought Annie's face to mind, recalling how calmly she had acted. She was really something else - different.

She started talking to him on day one, and assumed he was a friend from then on. She hadn't been turned off him by the damned rumours either. That had been unexpected enough, but then she had helped him out of that very bad spot, with those drugs put into his locker. He still didn't know who had done that the first time, when he had only just escaped being expelled. Even now, he didn't know who was trying to get him in trouble. If not for Annie, he would be up shit creek. He didn't want to turn her off him by letting on about his home life.

He couldn't see why she bothered with Abbie Carson, though. She'd been persistently rude to Annie since they'd met. Abbie had been alright to start, but ever since she had joined Gail Conte's little clique, she had become just like the rest of them. Just another Hell's Angel, as he had begun calling Gail's group. Control freak Gail liked to dictate what her friends could and couldn't do.  All her friends, and their's, had to be well off or have access to a supply of money from some source. Gail had told Abbie to ditch him once she learnt that he never had spare.

He'd been angry back then, but not enough to try to get money to waste on those users. Particularly to get it illegally, in spite of what a lot of people thought.

Staying at school was important to him. It was his only chance to become something better than his no-hoper of a father. At least he wasn't relying on his father to pay the school fees. His mother was doing that much for him, even if she never tried to see him anymore.

He didn't want to admit to feeling jealous at how Annie spoke of her parents, who weren't super-rich, but he judged them to be fairly well off. If it wasn't for Mr Cato at the milk bar, who paid him to work there, and also gave him groceries that were just at the end of their best by date, he might have been hauled off by Human Services to a foster home. It might have been better, but someone still needed to look out for his old man.

For the last couple of months though, he had been deemed an independent minor. His father had no say over what he did anymore, and he could if he wanted, tell his father where to go. He had been allowed to start getting youth allowance, even though he was still only fifteen. That meant that his father no longer received the family allowance, and be able to wager or drink it away. The Department checked up on him periodically, but he was looking after himself, eating well enough, and doing his best to keep most of the house clean, as well as his clothes and himself. In fact, he was looking after the person who should have been nurturing him.

Despite all that, the police were often around, asking him questions about local misdemeanours, petty robberies, and drugs. Somehow, he had got a reputation for those things when all he had ever done was try to beg food from the supermarket when he had been much younger. And if they weren't there to see him, they were around to see his father.

Martin had never been sure where his father got his money from, or what jobs he took on. Nor did he want to know. He certainly hadn't had a regular job for the past five years – ever since his mother had walked out. Somehow though, he still had enough money to get drunk on.

Such depressing thoughts occupied Martin until he was nearly home. When he turned into his street, he saw a police car waiting outside his house.

*What now?* He was half tempted to keep walking and not go home, but he was trying to act like a normal citizen who had nothing on his conscience. He shrugged and walked towards the car and wasn't surprised when the two occupants in their flak jackets and high-vis gear got out.

"Martin," one greeted. It was one he'd met often before, Constable Parnell. "A word with you?"

Martin stopped beside them. "Okay, what is it?"

"Where have you been?"

"School."

"Does it usually take you this long to get home?"

"No, I often get home later. I try to wait until my father has collapsed for the night."

They knew that too, since the local cops seemed to slow down and give him the once over when he was out late – just walking.

"Can we go inside rather than talk out here?"

Martin merely shrugged. The neighbours would get talking either way, and he probably didn't have the option to refuse unless he wanted them to think he was hiding something. He went to the front door, but when he used his key he found it was already unlocked. That must mean his father was home, since he'd gone out early and Martin had locked the house when he'd left.

He went in, expecting the usual greeting of, "That you, boy?" – if his father was conscious. When he didn't, Martin dropped his school bag in the hallway and demanded, "So, what is it that you want to talk about?"

He wasn't going to act like he wanted them there and offer coffee or anything.

"Where were you last night?" Parnell asked, while his off sider glanced around.

"Here. Eventually."

"From about what time?"

"Midnight."

"What about before that?"

"Walking about – in the park, by the river, between here and there. May I ask why?"

"Were you alone?"

"Of course. Your mates see me often enough, always by myself."

"Did you see anyone else around in the park?"

"The usual. Joggers, a couple who were parked and involved. I keep clear of the other types. What is this about?"

"Where's your father? Is he here?"

"Don't know. Thought he was because the front door was open. I'll have a look."

"Mind if I look with you?" Parnell asked, but it was a statement.

"Why not? I've nothing to hide."

Martin first went to the room his father kept his stuff in. He checked the far side of the bed as well, in case the slob had fallen off the bed. He checked all the other rooms, while the second constable checked outside. That one returned and asked, "Do you have a key to the garage?"

"It's never locked. The only thing in there is an old heap that blew its engine last week and piles of junk."

Simply by the constable maintaining eye contact, Martin got the hint to go find the key. He went to the kitchen, took a bowl from on top of the fridge, found the car's keys on a ring, and indicated the garage key.

"That one opens the side door. The big door has to be opened from inside."

Even though he had done nothing illegal, Martin seemed to feel the hand of the law on his neck. To try to seem unworried, he went to the kitchen sink to get himself a glass of water. His throat was dry.

The constable was back in moments. "There is a new lock on the door. This key doesn't work it."

"In that case, I don't know where the key is. You can try any that are in that bowl. Otherwise you will need to ask my father." He was trying to keep his voice calm and even, but he knew he'd failed, and expected the next statement.

"We would like you to accompany us to the station."

It wasn't worth resisting. He simply grabbed his school bag, and locked the house. On the way to the car, he saw the neighbours curtains twitch and knew the gossip was already getting around.

While Martin sat in the police car, he wondered yet again who kept telling the police he was doing something illegal. It was the same kind of nastiness as having drugs put in his locker at school.

Even when they arrived at the station and put him into a room, they didn't enlighten him. He was simply told to stay there, and warned of consequences if he didn't. It was a long time before anyone came, and by then he had resorted to reading more of the book he had to read for English. He had questions based on the book to complete, but he didn't think he'd have a chance to do them too. He hoped they would turn up soon. He needed to use the men's room, and he could do with something to eat.

His phone began to vibrate and he looked at it. Annie? What did she want? He cancelled the call. A short time later, it beeped and he read the message. 'Have more info on scout house. Will call again later.'

That matter was so unrelated to his current situation that he didn't care. He turned his phone off. It would need charging soon anyway.

He recognised the detective who entered when it was nearly 10 pm. Following him was his off-sider, Kelly, who had a plate of sandwiches and a can of lemonade. He put those down on the table with a faint grin. Martin didn't wait to begin eating.

The older detective glared at Kelly, who merely said, "Boys that age are always hungry."

"I was, thank you," Martin agreed, when he had swallowed his mouthful.

"I'll come back in a few minutes," the older detective decided.

Martin finished the food, and asked Kelly about a quick trip to the men's room.

Kelly was smart, Martin decided. The food had put him in a more cooperative mood for when his superior returned.

The first question was, "Do you have an adult you wish to have with you?"

"I'm assuming that you still don't have a clue where my father is."

"Other than your father. Is your mother available?"

"No. She went off years ago and I haven't seen her since. Do I have to have someone?"

"You are still a minor," the detective persisted.

Martin gave a mirthless chuckle. "Actually, I am a liberated minor. My father no longer has any say over me. I support myself, look after myself."

"Who owns the house where you are staying?"

"Actually, I do. It used to belong to my mother, but when she divorced my father, she had ownership transferred to me."

"Then why don't you have your father kicked out?"

"I dunno…" Martin said, but thought, *They wouldn't understand.*


"We are applying for a warrant to search your property, or we can forego that if you give us permission."

"You didn't have to keep me here for ages to do that."

"No, that was for your own protection, and we were under the impression your father owned the property."

"Protection? From who?"

"Associates of your father. Do you know who he is working for?"

"No."

"Anyone he works with?"

"No."

"Do you know what's in the garage?"

"No. That lock they mentioned wasn't on it two weeks ago. I went in there just after school went back to get some old dog stuff."

"What was in it then?"

"Just the same old junk as always."

"We will take you back with us, to have a look around."

His father was back, because the lights were on in the kitchen and his bedroom. Martin let the policemen follow him in and do what they intended.

"Shit, boy! What have you done now?"

"More like what have you done, you old sot. They have a search warrant for this place."

Kevin Kemple stood up from the table, banging it as he did. The remains of a hamburger placed back on its wrapping on the table.

Martin judged that he wasn't completely sober, but not as soaked as normal by that time of night. Anyone could have told he was alarmed by the intrusion, but he was quick to claim, "I have nothing here to interest you," while giving his son a sideways glance. "Sure, go ahead, check his room. He keeps saying he's independent now. I don't have to do anything to help him."

"Just remember, old man. That goes both ways." Martin hid the alarm he now felt.

"We would like the key to the garage."

"Do you coppers ever introduce yourselves?" Kemple demanded.

"I'm Senior Detective Tony Mendes," the older of the two police officers supplied. "The garage key?"

As Martin had done earlier, he went to the bowl on the fridge and tossed the ring of keys onto the table.

"None of those keys will open the new lock on the door."

"Then get him to tell you where it is,"Kemple said, pointing to Martin.

"Just cut the lock," Martin proposed. "If he won't give you the key, I can't help you."

Later, Martin decided that the police had not considered either him or his father to be dangerous. Ok, he was big for fifteen, but still not the size of Mendes or his mate Frank Kaspersky. His father was an overweight, unfit slob – more of a danger to himself in a fight. If the two detectives had expected trouble, they would have bought reinforcements.

As it was, Kaspersky went ahead to search the house while Mendes watched Kemple and Martin in the kitchen. The former went back to his hamburger, as if unworried.

When the bolt cutters arrived with a constable from the local station, Kaspersky had finished his search, and returned to the kitchen with a small bag of white tablets and a ziplock bag stuffed with notes. Kemple smirked. Martin felt the blood drain from his face.

Mendes had the constable follow him outside, bringing Kemple. Kaspersky sat at the table where Kemple had been, and pushed the greasy paper away.

"I'm surprised. Your father seems to have found a good take-away place."

In spite of the pending trouble, Martin managed a faint grin. "He won't cook for himself, and he thinks vegetables and healthy food are for weaklings. Yet, leave anything that looks like take-away or junk food, and he'll eat it."

"What do you eat?" Kaspersky was curious about the youngster. He'd paled when he'd seen the drugs, but was not showing signs of intending to bolt.

"The same. Except I use a plate. He probably thinks I brought that for myself. He leaves the rabbit food in the fridge."

Martin tried not to look at the bag of tablets, but he had to ask, "Where did you find them?"

"You don't know?" Kaspersky asked, sceptically.

"No, or I would have junked them the instant I saw them."

"Indeed?"

Some of the calm that he had been trying to project deserted

Martin. "You will no doubt believe what you want to, but for the record, I don't take drugs, make drugs, hide them, deliver them or sell them."

"These, and the money, were in a box under a loose board in your room," Kaspersky decided to confirm. "Did you know of that place?"

"Yeah. I stopped using it when that fat slob outside, pinched the money I'd been saving."

"So, are you accusing your father of putting them there? Why would he do that?"

"I'm not accusing him," Martin said, trying to be fair. "But since I told no one of the place, and he's the only other person likely to know of it, either he did, or he told someone of that place. Why I don't know, but his smirk suggested he knew the stuff was there."

"I heard that there was some trouble with drugs at your school," Kaspersky commented. "Your name was mentioned."

"I wasn't involved in that."

A sound from outside made Kaspersky rise, listening intently and instinctively going for his gun. The sound of a high powered car taking off had him running outside.

Martin sprinted after the detective, wondering what had first alerted the man. A light was streaming from inside the garage and in its light were two prone figures. He hesitated, not sure if he should go near the victims. Then he recalled what he had learnt at a first aid course the previous year. The constable was nearest, and he knelt to feel for a pulse and breathing. Feeling both, all else he saw was a bleeding head wound.

Kaspersky had first checked out the garage, and then run to kneel by his superior. His intake of breath, and immediate placing his hand into an area of blood caused Martin to say, "I'll fetch something."

He had never run faster, and quickly brought back two pillow slips that had been in the linen cupboard for years. He was rolling them into a wad as he returned to give them to the detective.

"Keep pressure on that!" Kaspersky directed, quickly wiping his hand on the grass before phoning for assistance. It was only then that Martin realised that his father was nowhere around.

"How was Jackson?" Kaspersky asked tersely.

"Oh, head wound, but breathing," Martin said. "Not bleeding too much."

The ambulance arrived quickly, along with another two police cars. Martin was glad to let the paramedics take over and back away. His father had really done it this time, getting in with people who thought nothing of knifing someone or bashing them over the head. He couldn't see his father doing either. Punching, yes, or kicking, but that was all.

For the moment, no one was paying him any attention and he wanted to be out of the way. He turned and hurried inside, with his gut feeling like it was about to eject its contents. He felt horribly alone, having no one to turn to, and wanting to cry like a baby. He had prided himself on being independent, but the downside was that he would have to face all this alone. The police would find it hard to believe that he knew nothing about this, or the drugs that were still sitting there in front of him. Had there been drugs in the garage? It seemed like it had to be.

He took a can of Pepsi from the fridge and sipped it slowly. His stomach settled, and he fought the urge to put his head on his arms and go to sleep. They would be taking him in – that was for sure.

"Ah, there you are." The lilting voice of DC Kelly woke Martin from a doze.

"So, you're here too, are you? Isn't there any other crime going on tonight?" Martin said sourly.

"Probably. However, I am glad to see that you are not adding to it."

"What do you mean?"

"The brass out there thought you'd run off, even though Frank told them how you had helped with Mendes."

Martin shrugged and sipped his now flat drink.

"I was impressed by how you handled that other matter last week. How are you now?"

All he could do was shake his head, and try to force the images from his mind. It seemed that Kelly understood.

"What's happening outside?" Martin asked.

"The forensic team is going over the garage. Mendes and Jackson have gone off to the hospital. I was told to find you and bring you to the station."

"I wish you guys would leave me alone."

"Well, I don't have to take you straight away. Frank heard a hotted up car taking off. A car that might have been that one, was seen heading back towards the city. It was a two door sedan, so Frank thinks your father—"

"Call him Kemple. I am never going to consider that bastard my father ever again."

"Okay, we think Kemple took off on foot rather than in the car. Any idea where he'd go?"

"No, sorry."

"Let's drive around for a while, okay?"

"Whatever," Martin agreed, forcing himself up. "Did they find anything in the garage?"

"Some stolen stuff, bulky items. Tony might have seen something else in there before he was attacked."

"Drugs, do you think?" Martin persisted.

"I really can't say," Kelly admitted. "Are you coming?"

"Yeah, alright." Martin caught up his school bag on the way out.

"Do you need that?"

"It has my wallet, phone and iPad in it. Plus my school stuff. All that I have that is of any value. I don't need some opportunist to sneak in while your mates are outside."

"All right then, come on."

At least they went out to an unmarked police car, as if he were just being picked up to go to a friend's place. The neighbours were out in force, staring at the lights in his back yard, trying to see what was going on. He knew he'd been recognised, as he waited for Kelly to get in the driver's seat and open the door for him.

"Will I be allowed back here later?"

"We'll see," Kelly said neutrally. "There might be things we need to ask you."

"I guess so." Martin guessed it wouldn't be just a nice chat, but an inquisition.

"Does Kemple have any favourite places?"

"I really don't know – maybe wherever he gets his beer, does his betting, or manages to find a prostitute who isn't too revolted by him."

"That's a start. How fast can Kemple run?"

"Depends on the prod. I would say he couldn't really run very far at all."

"That's my view too. Assuming he wasn't in the car. Okay, why don't I drive around a few places, and you keep your eyes out for him?"


Although they drove around the shopping centre, several hotels, and the park, where lots of people were about, they saw no sign of Kevin Kemple.

Martin decided that only a very small part of him was relieved. Most of him wanted the bastard put in jail.

"I'm going to change all the locks on the house," he blurted. "And toss all his stuff into the garage when you guys are finished in there."

"You could opt to stay elsewhere," Kelly suggested.

"No damn way! The house belongs to me – not to him."

"Ah, but isn't he your guardian?"

"He's a nobody. I'm an independent minor – I can support myself. I would be doing better if he wasn't freeloading off me."

"Then, I think you should do what you suggested," Kelly told him seriously. "And if he comes back causing trouble, you can apply for a restraining order against him."

It was the first positive idea he'd had since his current nightmare began. He'd just hope they still didn't intend to arrest him.

By the time Kelly stopped cruising around, Martin was dozing off. He woke when they parked at the police station. He grabbed his bag and followed Kelly inside, where there was more activity than he expected.

Kelly shepherded him past the information windows in the foyer, and into the back areas where they came to a room full of desks. Martin slumped into a chair that Kelly pulled out,

and he hardly heard, "Wait here, will you Martin?"
   *What else could he do?*

Martin rested his head on his arms, but watched Detective Kelly approach a tall, white haired, straight-backed man. That man, casually dressed, was talking to two dark clad figures. He tried to listen more intently, but all he could make out were two soft American accented voices, and a growling murmur from the tall man.

During the next few hours, in between periods of dozing, Martin answered questions from various policemen. Most of the subjects, Martin had no knowledge of. One brought over photographs, and Martin rubbed his eyes to see them better. His mind was almost too tired to think, but then he did see a face he recognised.

"That's like a guy I saw outside the back of the school."

A few others he'd paused at, thinking them somewhat familiar, but he wasn't sure. The detective prodded him about some of them.

"This one? You've seen him?"

"I think I saw him tonight, somewhere around the shops or one of the pubs. At first glance, he looked like Kemple. When he turned, I realised it wasn't."

"What about this one?" The detective indicated another.

Martin had to shake his head.

"This one?"

"Yeah. I do know him. He works for Mr Gilroy, my cousins' stepfather. What did he do to be in your rogue's gallery?"

"Possibly nothing. These are some people we've had under observation. Any others you were unsure about?"

Martin indicated another. "That one. I think he was amongst the gawkers at my place when I left. I don't think he's one of the neighbours."

That, Martin decided, was of particular interest. The detective went over to the phone and gave someone orders.

Kelly came over with a cup of hot chocolate. "I've arranged a place for you to sleep if you want. I will come and get you if you can go home."

"Is it in a cell?" Martin yawned.

"No, it's a room upstairs where we sleep if we are too damned tired to drive home, or have to stay on call."

"Right now, I would have settled for a cell."


Martin was woken at five in the morning, by Kelly.

"Wake up lad. I'm to take you home."

"Oh, great! Have they finished there?"

"I believe so. Though there will be an officer on duty there during the day."

"How come?"

"Mainly a precaution, or in case Kemple comes home."

"I don't suppose I can get him to ring my school and tell them I won't be in?"

"You could ask – on the grounds of a family emergency."

"Huh! More like a major family embarrassment."

After running his hands through his hair, and grabbing his bag, Martin said he was ready. He wanted a shower, and fresher clothes. He did have one spare uniform, but he really didn't want to be at school that day.


The duty officer was young and quite friendly. He was to stay in the house, out of sight. Martin had to admit to himself that having the man there was a relief. If his father did come back, he'd get a nasty surprise. And it meant that he could go back to sleep for a few hours without worrying if anyone else would turn up.

Yet, soon after he had showered, changed into jeans and tee shirt, and eaten a bowl of cereal, he heard a car door slamming, and a car revving off. He and the constable raced outside. Martin stopped when he saw his father – clothing torn, and bleeding from multiple abrasions. The constable returned after trying to see the car.

Still just staring, Martin watched the constable check for a pulse.

"He's alive," was the verdict, before the constable phoned in to report and arrange an ambulance. When that and a police car turned up, Martin decided that at least, most of the neighbours had left for work or to take kids to school. Though as he thought that, he glanced up to see the Bellfield School bus pass the end of his street. He scowled. As well he had decided to stay home. Though he wouldn't be able to meet Annie either, and that had become the best part of his day.

Too much had happened to him, Martin decided, for him to be content just sitting around. He should try to get to school, but someone on that bus would know he lived up the street where the activity was. Word would get around and the teachers would start eyeing him again. No doubt worse rumours would be going around by Monday. What he needed now was to get out and walk. Clear his head.

"Do I have to stay here?" he asked the constable once the ambulance and escorting police car had gone. The question was a test. He still wasn't sure if the constable was meant to watch him too.

"Going to school?" he was asked.

"No. I just want to walk."

"Keep your phone on then," the constable advised. "Do you need to call up and say you won't be at school?"

"We are meant to. I don't care. I did think about asking you to, but I don't want Gill thinking you arrested me."

"What's he now? Headmaster?"

With surprise, Martin answered, "Deputy Head. Acting in for Mr Allen while he's away."

"How about I mention a family emergency and you being upset?"

"Would you? I really don't want Gill on my back any more than he already is."

When the call had been made, Martin asked, "Did you go to Bellfield?"

"Some years back, yes."

Since the constable, Harry Trent, was being friendly, Martin asked, "Why have they put you here?"

"The higher ups are not sure if anyone intends to come back. They certainly didn't expect Kemple to be dumped here. That might have been a ploy to scare you."

"Surely the ones who were here took what they wanted?"

"If they did, why beat up—"

"Him? He deserved it. Do you think they wanted the drugs they found in my room? That fat slob surely knew about them. He looked like he expected me to be arrested."

"It might be a possibility," Trent admitted. "We don't know why they were in your garage, or if they took anything when they fled. It does look like they were storing stolen goods there."

"Do you think they might want to look in the house?" Martin asked. "Should I stay here?"

"I have no orders to keep you locked up here," Trent assured him.

"If they come here when I'm out, can you handle them?"

"I'll have back up, but you will need to keep alert. They might try for you. So, like I said, keep your phone on. Call if you see anything that worries you."

"It hasn't much charge. I was going to do that yesterday."

Once he was out of the house, Martin finally felt he could breathe. Yet at the same time, his mind had not stopped circling around the question of who his father had got mixed up with. Would those unknowns really try to get him for some reason? And why had his father put drugs in his room? Was it to get him taken out of the way? So he wouldn't find the stolen stuff? If it was, his father had gone too far.

Martin decided that he no longer owed his father anything. He had to have planted the drugs in his room, and that was the last straw. His thoughts hardened into determination. He was going to do what he had suggested – get new locks for the front and back door and when he could, he'd get them for the windows too. Then, if the police didn't keep his father in custody once he was well enough to be questioned, Kevin Kemple would wish they had.

As he walked up to the main road, Martin wasn't too deep in thought that he didn't notice the parked car. To his eye, it was an unmarked police car, parked down from his house where they had a good view of both ends of the street as well. He pretended not to notice, but he gave it a quick glance before he turned the corner, and it didn't seem like it was going to follow him. Though that didn't mean they wouldn't report he had left.

Maybe they hadn't believed he had known nothing of the drugs in his room. Perhaps they wanted to see if he went to his supplier to report the loss. He kept a watch out for cars following him, or circling the block, or for people walking behind him. Well, he didn't know any more than he had told them.

He straightened from his walking slouch when he neared the shops. He'd go to Bunnings Hardware, they had a good range and he might need tools. The place was as busy as usual, judging by the rows of cars in their carpark. He moved to cross the road between the rows, and glancing to look for cars and people following him, he almost walked into an old looking woman. He apologised, and put his mind back on his task, but the oddity of that woman, carrying a kid's plastic drawstring toilet bag, made him shake his head. That's when he caught movement in the corner of his eye. The tall figure of Borton, his step-uncle's driver, was walking towards him from behind him to his left. Though it didn't seem as if the man had recognised him yet. Instead of continuing into the store, Martin ducked behind the nearest car, and used it and others to cover him until the man was ahead of him. Normally, he wouldn't have worried, the guy usually gave him a hard time, but he was used to that. This time, it was because the police had been watching him.

While he watched for a chance to dash across the last section of the access road, he saw the trolley rattling towards Borton, who was paying it no heed. A woman dashed into view, chasing it, but she didn't reach it till a moment after it hit Borton.  Then you could hear her apologising loudly, asking if he was hurt. Martin grinned and took his chance to dive across the road and trot to the store.


It didn't take Martin long to find what he wanted, and pay for the locks with his ATM card. They were expensive, and didn't leave him with much in his account, but his allowance was due in two days. He considered the cost a small investment in his safety. With the two locks in a small cardboard box, he was about to saunter out until a hissed, "Stay back, boy!" and an outstretched arm stopped him.

He looked at the short woman, who he was sure was the one who had chased the trolley earlier, and wondered who she was to think she could command him. Her accent wasn't Australian, his best guess was European of some sort.

"Have you been following me?" Martin asked in a low voice.

"Not exactly. I was watching him, and when he saw you, wondering why he began watching you."

"Why watch him?"

"He is a person of interest to me," the woman told him.

"Hey! You were at the police station yesterday – talking to

the tall bloke. But you sounded American then and your hair was different."

The woman laughed. "I didn't expect you to notice me. You looked too petrified of being put in jail." Her accent had reverted to American, and the dissembling was faintly amusing.

"Yeah, I was. I really didn't think they were convinced that I wasn't a supplier."

"They weren't, possibly still aren't, but you wanting to avoid ferret face out there, backs up my theory."

"What theory."

"Shh!"

Martin looked out and saw two men that he knew to be detectives, leading Borton off.

"Okay, it's probably safe enough for you to go out now."

"Are you a police person?"

"Ah, no...I'm more of a consultant."

"Are you interested in me or my father?" Martin decided to be blunt.

"Should I be? I have been looking at known associates of a number of people. There was a robbery a couple of days ago. The recovery of a particular stolen object is my main interest."

"Oh." Martin decided he'd not be told any more. "You said something about a theory before."

"Yes, well, while I was hanging around the police station, I was innocently eavesdropping. I saw you there, and decided to add my dime's worth."

"About what?"

"Them finding stuff in your room, in a supposedly hidden place, when you had already said your old man knew of it."

"Yeah! If he knew of it, I'd not use it. If I was hiding anything with value – he'd pinch it."

"Exactly! So are you planning to make two more secure hidey holes?"

Martin glanced at the box he was carrying. "No, I am going to change the locks on my place to keep my father out."

"Good on you. Want a hand? My usual job is security expert. I might be able to offer some ideas you haven't thought of."

"I should be right, but...yeah, since you are offering, I'd appreciate your help." Truth was, the woman intrigued him.

Martin listened, watched and learnt. The woman did indeed know what needed doing. She showed him how to reinforce around the lock, and also the hinges. He had never considered the latter to be a security weakness. Then she gave him inventive ways to stop the windows being forced open, and little alarms to warn him if someone tried. What he liked best was that she didn't treat him like a kid. She let him install the lock, with only minor advice. She reminded him of an older Annie Jamieson, or perhaps in time, Annie would become as confident as this woman. Before she left, she told him, and the silently observing constable, that neither of them had seen her.

Somehow, she had been like a fresh breeze blowing through the house. Memories of the uncertainties of the previous couple of days had receded and his confidence in being able to face down the snobs and bullies at school had returned. He was going to need that.

<u>Chapter 6</u>

Martin looked around his house and took a deep breath. Now, he would be able to come home and do his homework, rather than having to disappear at breaks to get it done in the small room he was permitted to use. Though that usually kept him from those who wanted to belittle or discredit him.

After lunch, brought in by the constable coming on duty, Martin had a satisfying afternoon taking all his father's possessions from his room to the garage. He made sure he locked the side door with a new lock. When he was finished, he brought out his schoolbooks, and checked his homework and assignment due list. He set to writing a history essay, and was only disturbed by the constable, who had been told Kevin Kemple had regained consciousness, and would be able to be questioned later in the evening.

Martin only shrugged and said, "He'd better not try to tell any more lies about me."

Later, he wondered if his father had done that, for Detective Kelly and his senior partner, Kaspersky, came to the door. He let the constable open it and finished the paragraph he was up to in his essay.

"What now?" he asked, aware they were watching him from the depths of the two sagging arm chairs. "Did that fat, lying slob try to convince you that I don't know what I am doing half the time?"

Kelly smiled at the accuracy of the thrust. "He did try to convince us that you were a chip off the old block. Reckons that you spend half your time stoned or drunk."

"He's the one that's always stoned or drunk, and wouldn't know if I was alive or dead. I don't want to be anything like him."

"Do you know, he reckons you are wagging school half the time and doesn't know why they haven't kicked you out?"

"I have not!"

"Calm down, lad," Kaspersky suggested. "We checked with the school and know you rarely miss a day. Why do you make him think you were?"

"It keeps him paranoid that I know what he gets up to."

Both detectives laughed at his candid admission. "Do you?"

"Hell no. He's stupid if he believes it."

"And I don't believe you are, since the school says you are passing your classes satisfactorily, even if not with top grades," Kaspersky told him. "However, at the moment, if the wrong people think you know anything..."

"I hope the slob didn't let that on to any one – but I had the locks on the house changed. Anyway, did the powers at school air all their doubts about me?"

"Instances were mentioned," Kelly admitted. "However, we assured them that we do not consider you to have been in any way involved in the drug business."

"Does that mean I don't need to worry about you coming to arrest me?"

"If you keep out of trouble."

"So why did you come?"

Kaspersky got down to business. "A couple of points you might be able to help us with. Have you any knowledge of Kemple's movements on Tuesday and Wednesday?"

"He's usually still snoring when I leave for school, and I try not to get home too early – but, Tuesday he got back about 10pm and he wasn't as drunk as usual. I didn't actually see him on Wednesday. Didn't hear him snoring, but I assumed he was passed out like normal. I wasn't going to check as I went off to school. That night, he came in around 10 again. That's all I can say, sorry."

"Does your father have a mobile phone?" Kaspersky asked.

"Yeah, but if he didn't have it on him, I don't know where it is. I took all his stuff outside earlier and didn't see it."

"Do you know his number?"

"Nuh! I think he uses a prepaid one. I'm pretty sure he had his original number disconnected. I found unpaid phone bills."

"You've been very helpful," Kaspersky told him as he stood up.

"Are you going to keep him locked up?" Martin asked. "Did he bash that constable?"

"He hasn't admitted to anything, but he had to have seen who did, if he didn't. We have charged him as accessory. He also matches the description of a man involved in a robbery two days ago, and some of the stuff we removed from your garage has been identified as stolen."

"Was the stuff in the garage from that robbery?"

"It might have been – we are still checking the waybills on the items we recovered," Kaspersky told him. "We will hold him until the initial hearing, unless someone posts bail for him."

"It won't be me," Martin declared.

"We'll be off, then," Kaspersky announced. "Thanks for talking to us."

Martin worked on Sundays, at the milk bar which was in convenient walking distance of the nearby sports precinct and the Riverpark. He hadn't forgotten to keep alert for potential trouble, and also wondered if the police were watching him anyway. He was almost at the shop when he heard, "You! Boy! Kemple's kid."

He turned to see a bulky man, taller than his father, trotting his way.

"Where's Kemple got to?" was the demand. "Bastard's not answering his phone."

"Who are you?" Martin demanded.

"He's meant to be working for me."

Martin considered what to say, and decided the truth was best. "I have no idea about his phone. But he was bashed unconscious on Friday night and dumped at home. Police took him to hospital since they wanted to question him."

The man began looking around as if he thought the police were watching him. That news wasn't what he wanted to hear. He abruptly stalked off. Martin followed his progress, and saw an old looking woman trot after him with two take-away coffees in a cardboard holder. She had a plastic drawstring bag dangling from her wrist, and he belatedly recognised her from when he'd gone to the shops.

With a shrug, he went into the shop and began his usual first task of sweeping the shop and store room, and wondering if he should mention the man to Kelly or Kaspersky. Not unexpectedly, his cousins turned up half an hour later, and began their usual baiting until Mr Cato, told them to leave if they weren't buying anything.

Martin was fetching another slab of drinks for the fridge when two of the Hell's Angels arrived. On seeing them through the shop window, he began to hum the 'Death March' at their stupidity.

When Claire and Gail came in, they didn't look his way, just murmured about the 'maid service'. They went out again once they had their 'girl' magazines.

He doubted they were aware that their conversation outside could be heard inside. Martin, continuing to stock shelves, heard when Abbie arrived on foot. It was obvious to him that she was in a right snit, and wasn't confiding in her friends. She was trying to borrow a phone to call with, and when they didn't agree, came storming into the shop.

"Do you have money for the phone?" Abbie demanded. He paused a while before turning around, as if just realising she was talking to him.

"Where's yours? Did your folks confiscate it?"

"None of yours, Kemple. Well, do you?"

Martin debated with himself for a moment before feeling for the right coins in his pocket and tossing them to her. She didn't thank him, but he hadn't expected her to. He went back to flattening boxes, and heard occasional words of her phone conversation without even trying.

"Stupid, stupid, pampered princess," he muttered to herself. "She doesn't realise when she is well off."

He ignored her as she went out. Obviously it was no use reminding her that she wasn't meant to see Adam. He went back to checking dates on the refrigerated stuff, until he heard a hotted up car drive up and stop outside. He spied Adam getting out of the front passenger seat of the two door sedan, and his cousins greeting the driver. Tory Michaelson had only left school the previous year, but if he could afford a car like the convertible outside, he had to be doing something illegal.

Abbie had better hope he behaved himself.

# Episode 6

# Mysteries Deepen

## (Annie's POV)

### Chapter 1

While walking to school, I told Martin about the visit of the policeman to Naomi's place the previous Thursday and what I had learnt relating to the find at the scout place. He considered it all, but summed up my own feeling.

"Not much more we can do."

After a while, I commented, "I heard there were police and ambulance in your street Friday morning."

"Yeah. It would have been quite a spectacle for the school bus sticky beaks," Martin agreed.

"I was hoping it had nothing to do with you."

"Useless hope, I'm afraid. So what is everyone saying was going on?"

I laughed. "The worst was that you killed your father in a drug fuelled rage."

"Would need to be drug fuelled to want to do that. I've fantasised about it often enough. However, I have more interesting things I want to do with my life than being in jail for doing him in."

"I should think so. Like what?"

"Communications," Martin summarised.

"I want to be an architect like my dad," I admitted.

"At least you have a dad who has a legal job."

"I gather yours doesn't."

"Huh! I don't really want to know where he gets his money from. As it was, I spent most of Friday at the police station, and the week end with a police house guest."

"They didn't think you did anything?" I was dismayed.

"They said it was for my protection."

"I wasn't going to ask, but well, what did happen?"

"The stupid bastard has been up to something. Don't know what, but he must have pissed someone off because he was bashed and dumped on the nature strip."

"How is he?"

"Alive."

"And?"

"And I hope the police lock him up and lose the key."

"Won't that mean they will put you in with foster parents or something?"

I didn't understand why Martin began laughing.

"No, you see my mum transferred the house to me. So I have a place to live. And I get an allowance, so I can look after myself."

"Wow! I can't imagine doing that."

"I hope you never have to," Martin said, sobering.


The idea kept me quiet for a while and it occurred to me that Martin had actually paid me a compliment. He didn't open up to anyone at school as far as I knew.

"You know, just knowing what really happened, instead of getting Gail's made up stories, is such a delicious secret."

"Does she stir you up?"

"Yeah, but she's just trying to feel important, or so my dad says. I have no intention of telling her what you told me. I will just smile pityingly at her and shake my head at her delusions."

Martin laughed at the idea. "She'll just get worse you know."

"Probably, but at least I have made some good friends with Naomi and Karen, and you. And I don't think they will let Gail change their minds or yours. So, I am better off than when I started at Bellfield. In any case, I will probably be at yet another school next year."

"You're amazing, you know that?"

"Of course I do. So, when might you come and visit Lucky-Pup again? I think my dad wants to check you out and I reckon you might like an occasional free feed you don't have to put together."

"I'll let you know."


We were almost at the school's back gate when I asked, "Was Abbie hanging out with Gail and Claire yesterday?"

"For a bit, then Gail got uppity with her and she left."

"Alone?"

"No, she went with Adam. Why?"

"Just wondering. Abbie has been acting odd since she visited my place."

"If you ask me, that lot are all idiots."

"Because they aren't meant to be seeing the boys?"

"Yeah. Actually, that goes both ways. Gerry was really pissed off after you went."

"Why? Did the penny finally drop?"

Martin laughed. "Like a brick. He and Tom took off like the cops were after them. They probably hadn't thought about the responsibilities of being adult, just the perks."

"What about Gail and Claire?"

"You did them a favour. Not long after the cousins left, a cop car did pull up."

"Had someone reported them hanging out?"

Martin shrugged. "Maybe, but they were looking for Abbie."

"Did you say anything?"

"No, I was inside stacking shelves. Gail reckoned they hadn't seen her."

I told myself that surely Abbie was all right, and she would be in class.

Gail, Clare and Helen, were in a tight group outside when

I went to put stuff in my locker. I guessed they were waiting for Abbie, but I wasn't interested in going near them. Just the tone of their whispers suggested they were in a mood that was not merely bitchy, but well on the way to venomous.

Abbie wasn't at homeroom, nor present for the first two periods. I didn't expect to see her at all that day, and I was worried about her.

I joined Karen and Naomi at the break and listened as the topic of the policeman's visit was discussed. Karen was, apparently, also a scout. My mind went back to the missing Maude. She'd had no one to help her after her accident, so where did the supposed cousin come from?

"Earth to Annie," Karen said pointedly. I jerked around.

"I said, did you see the picture in today's paper of Mad Maude?"

"No. My dad grabs it on his way out. What did the article say?"

"That the police are concerned for her safety, and if spotted to call the police."

Naomi added, "It also mentioned that her husband had been released from jail not long ago."

"Did it say what he had been inside for?"

"Can't you guess?" she teased. "Dealing drugs."

"Do you think that trap door thing in that room was his place to ditch stuff if he got visited by the police?" I ventured to say, as my imagination suggested a horrible possibility. What if the 'cousin' was actually her husband, and she had gone to be with him? Forgetting that he had been abusive.

"Annie has a soft spot for Maude," Naomi told Karen.

"Do you reckon she was innocent?" Karen asked me.

"I think people are willing to think she is a child killing monster," I blurted.

"It's pretty sure that she took those two kids," Karen insisted.

"I'm not arguing that. It's just that I don't think she would have killed her kids. She was looking after her two kids okay, even though she had no family to turn to. Then she has an accident, and her husband, who is not the kids father says she can't work anymore, or even look after herself. What if he got the authorities to take the kids, without her agreement?"

"Whoa there!" Karen said. "What are you getting at?"

"She was simple to start with, what if, in her addled state, she took the babies thinking they were hers? Both had been left unattended."

"But they found remains at the house," Naomi reminded me.

"There's no proof to say she put them there."

"You might be right Annie, but all that is in the past and done with. It's not like we can do anything about it now," Karen said.

"Yeah," I agreed glumly, thinking of Abbie. I wasn't even able to help a friend in trouble because I wasn't meant to know she was.

To my surprise, I saw Abbie coming out of the admin annex just before the end of break. Her cheeks were unusually red, and her expression unreadable. She went to the lockers, but had gone into our homeroom before the bell. We had English with Mrs Sutton next, and I had seen the teacher go in already. Naomi saw whcre I was looking. "I wonder what she got herself into."

I had a fairly good idea, but I only asked, "What do you mean?"

"Oh, I heard Gail saying something, but it didn't make sense. It just seemed like she was blaming Abbie for humiliating them."

"Makes a change from them blaming me," I said, but if my sudden suspicion was correct, they deserved what they got.

"Let's head in, huh?"

The bell went just as we'd finished at the lockers. Abbie and Mrs Sutton were talking in the classroom, but they finished then and Abbie nodded and turned away. She took a seat near the front.

The other Hell's Angels barged past us and went – quite deliberately – to seats well away from Abbie, but where she could see them. I began to edge towards the front, but Naomi pulled me back.

"Now isn't a good time to bc near Abbie, or to seem friendly towards her."

"But..."

"Trust me. They will just target you as well."

"Yeah, I guess."

Naomi was right, but something about Abbie was pulling at me.

When the bell went, I was ready to stand up and leave, but while the rest of the class hurried out, Abbie didn't get up. Her so called friends had left quickly, not even giving her a backwards look. I did, and I saw Abbie moving slowly.

"Come on, Annie," Karen nudged me. "I borrowed a ball to practice with."

She had heard me admit that I'd played some basketball at my last school. At the time, I had looked forward to playing, but right now, I wanted to help Abbie even though I couldn't think of a reason to go over. Maybe I will get a chance during the lunch break.

Half an hour after beginning, when what little skill I had was coming back to me, I saw Abbie walking quickly from the direction of the library towards the music prac rooms. That was also in the direction of the back gate. Was she trying to sneak out?

"I'll catch you later," I told my friends.

Naomi warned, "Don't catch a detention."

She had guessed what I planned, so I grinned.

Thanks to Martin, I now knew a few ways through to the back of the school. Most were out of bounds during school time but I risked using one now, so I just had to dive from beside one of the maintenance sheds to the back of the classrooms. I saw Abbie sitting on the ground, back to the wall, just out of sight. I trotted over next to her. Close, but not touching.

"Go away, charity case."

"No. It's quiet around here."

It wasn't. The classroom behind us had a wannabe guitarist torturing music.

"Why are you here?" Abbie demanded.

I shrugged. "You don't have to talk to me."

For a long time she didn't – just kept pulling up grass and

shredding it.

"Have you ever done anything absolutely stupid?" Abbie finally spoke.

"Yeah."

"What?"

"Well, I once barged into the wrong classroom."

"Why?"

I told her it had been two schools back when the class had been called out to have some injection. We'd left our books in class, but the bell had gone before the last of us could go back. We'd had to go get our stuff.

"I still blush, just thinking of it."

Abbie went back to shredding grass. "What I did, beats that."

"If you say so. Is it why Gail looks like she wants you to disappear?" I didn't look at her, just began to pick grass stalks and toss them away.

"Sort of. I just wanted to get away from home for a while. It was feeling like a prison. So I called Adam and he got his brother to drive and pick me up."

"I thought you—"

"Weren't meant to? Yeah, but ....."

"Did something horrible happen?" This time I did look at her. She was just staring at her knees. I reached for a dandelion flower, as a reason to brush against her. I had an image of an older boy and a sense of being groped but that wasn't what Abbie admitted.

"Yeah. The police found me there. I got taken to the police station. My dad was furious."

"I suppose he might have been," I agreed. "What happened then?"

"I had to go to court this morning."

Rather than ask details, I said, "Yep, that definitely tops anything I've done."

At that point in time, the tortured music ceased, and I heard a voice that sounded like Martin's, talking to a teacher. I nudged Abbie, and with a finger to my lips gestured that we should run along the back of the row of classrooms and get back to where we were meant to be. The brief touch gave me way too many impressions to concentrate on. It was enough to tell me that there was a lot more to Abbie's mood than she had just shared.

It was almost time for the bell, so I offered, "You can always call me if you feel like discussing the weather, or maths or stuff."

"I can't. Dad took my phone. Said he would be changing the number so the boys can't ring me."

"Landline?" I suggested.

"Dad has probably got the new housekeeper ready to stop me or listen in."

"Email?"

"Maybe – but he knows my email address."

"Make one up. A free one from Gmail or something. That's what I did for Facebook and places like that. Fairydust63@gmail.com."

"I might do that. I don't want to go on Facebook, Gail has probably left a hundred lethal messages on messenger."

We emerged, with no one paying us particular attention. I went to wash my hands, Abbie went off towards the lockers. Martin saw me and grinned. I'd have to thank him for running interference with the duty teacher. I owed him one.

Martin was lounging by the back gate, playing with his phone when I caught up to him. He was grinning.

"What's funny?"

"I think I know what got the Hell's Angels furious."

"What?"

"They all got dragged to the police station – my cousins included – and were given a severe warning about being seen together."

"Oh! Are your cousins blaming you?"

"It's a reflex action for them, but I said if I had wanted them locked up, I wouldn't have clarified your warning."

"Huh! The idiots." Well, that had proved my earlier idea correct.

We began walking. Martin pocketed his phone, and took out a tennis ball. He began bouncing it.

"Did Abbie open up to you?"

"Not a lot."

"I heard that Adam got hauled into court for seeing her."

"Now how would you hear that?" I asked. "You're hardly ever around at breaks and Adam hasn't been at school."

"Oh, I have ways."

"Your cousins?"

"Them? Hell no. The police don't gossip to the likes of them."

"Yeah, well, Abbie did too. She said her father was furious."

"Mr high and mighty probably was."

I recalled Naomi saying Martin had been friendly with Abbie before she joined Gail's little group.

The tennis ball hit a stone and bounced my way. I grabbed it and bounced it back to him.

"How come you are mostly inside at breaks? Have you a permanent detention?"

Martin grabbed the ball and stopped walking. "Who told you?"

"Um…" I realised what I had done. "I'm imagining things."

He reached out and touched my arm. I started getting more images than I wanted so I jerked away.

"I'm sorry," I told him.

"Hey, it's okay. When did you figure it out?"

I shrugged. "You nearly always seem to disappear."

"It's not detention, but I am allowed to use a small room near the staffroom when I need to catch up on work. I never could work at home, though now I can."

"Is that how you heard about Adam?"

Martin nodded and grinned. "Gill and some of the senior teachers were discussing whether to let him back."

"Did they mention Abbie?"

"Not that I heard."

"Oh, while I think of it, thanks for running interference today."

"What are friend's for? I saw you going off though I still don't know why you bother with Princess Abbie."

"She's okay."

"She's no better than the other holier than thou Hell's Angels."

"And you're a very lucky drug pusher."

"Hey! What do you mean?"

"Well, that's what everyone thinks, right?"

"I thought I had managed to convince everyone otherwise."

"Yes, but you've had a lot going on at home that you haven't talked about, and no one knows, right?"

"Yeah." Martin caught and held his ball.

"So has Abbie."

"Did she tell you?"

"Not exactly."

"Did she tell those cronies of hers?"

"I don't think so."

"Then what?"

I wanted to squirm. "Just some really freaky ideas that I got while wearing her shoes, or getting touched by her stuff."

Martin began to bounce the ball again, more slowly. I swiped it as it rose and bounced it myself.

"Like what?" he finally asked.

I shook my head, not wanting to admit to my annoying secret skill.

"Do you get ideas about me from my ball?"

"You ought to try out for the basketball team."

"So should you and don't change the subject."

I did anyway. "You changed the locks at your place."

His mouth dropped open and he grabbed my arm again. "That's incredible. How do you do it?"

I shook my head. "It's more like how do I not do it."

"Does anyone else know about this?"

"Not really." I mentally crossed my fingers. "Well, if Abbie stops to think, she might suspect."

In fact, I hoped she had forgotten, but there was that incident with the brochure that time. At least, so far, she hadn't said anything, or I would be a laughing stock right now. Perhaps Abbie didn't want to provoke any questions that she didn't want to answer.

I expected more questions from Martin, but we walked on in silence. He seemed to be thinking. Near where we usually parted company, he said, "Is that why you wanted Maude's stuff."

"Not exactly. I was getting images from stuff in the house. I don't think she did what they said. It's not proof though."

"Do you even know what she looks like? The papers only had an old photo."

"There was a newer one in today's paper. They still don't know where she is."

"You're worried about her," Martin realised. "But you don't even know her."

"Yeah, so what?"

"She could still be guilty."

"So might you. Am I wrong?"

"No...okay, I just had to say it. Have you ever been wrong?"

"I don't know. The freaky stuff hasn't been happening long."

"You got Maude's stuff back, you said."

"I haven't tried it again. There's probably other impressions on them now.  What I picked up was all old, anyway."

"When are they working on the house again?"

"I don't know for sure yet. I'll see if Dad has heard anything, or I can ring Naomi?"

"I think, I'll try to be there."

"Naomi was wondering..."

Not long after I had tired out Lucky-pup, my phone rang. I didn't recognise the number.

"Hello?"

"Hi Annie, it's Martin."

"Oh! Hi. What's up?"

"You know that photo in today's paper?"

"Yeah." There had only been one that I mentioned.

"I think I have seen her around."

"Really? Where?"

"The shops, and in River Park, when I was heading to work or just hanging around."

"Oh."

"Want to hang out and look for her?"

"I can't exactly carry around her box of stuff in the hope I see her."

What did I want? I had envisioned myself visiting her at the place where she officially lived. If we saw her, what should I do? She didn't know me and I didn't exactly want to turn her in either.

"Maybe we could find out where she is staying?" Martin suggested.

"I don't know. That detective said she went off with someone who reckoned she was his cousin. But the lady at the shops said she was the last of her family. That guy might be dangerous."

"And he might be dangerous to her," Martin countered.

"What could we do besides tell the police where she is?"

"It might be the best answer. Once I saw her with a bloke that knows my dad."

"Have you mentioned that to anyone?"

"Only about the bloke talking to me."

"Why don't you mention it then? They might find her... I can't help feeling she is on the run, but nothing was said suggesting she'd done anything wrong recently."

"I could. But we could still look out for her too?"

"Is that a date?"

"No, just a suggestion."

"Dad won't let me out when I have school next day. And he will probably want to check you out, like I said. What if I ask if you can come to tea tomorrow night?"

"Is that a date?" Martin asked with a chuckle.

"No, it's an invitation."

## Chapter 4

The box with Maude Delaney's special possessions kept drawing my attention. Essays for English were much less interesting. Lucky-pup's eyes followed me when I stood up from my desk. She had moved her floppy dog bed near to my feet.

The box had sat for several days as I intentionally put off trying for images, but if I was going to try and find Maude, to give these things back to her, I might be running out of time. I had already felt the images from the photo frame showing two happy little girls. Now, when I touched it, there was nothing. The frame had traces of powder, like they had tried for finger prints. I decided to clean it as much as I could. The decorative plastic had begun to darken with age, but a damp cloth removed the powder and dust.

There were many things in the box that I hadn't touched so I looked through and decided to bring out two tarnished silver mugs. Both were small, and the type people gave new mothers. Again, I felt nothing. Maybe they had been handled too much. I wasn't sure how to clean them up, so I went in search of Mum, and showed her my problem.

She surprised me. "They feel like solid silver."

I had thought they were only silver plated plastic. Mum tried rubbing one to see the inscription, but the tarnish didn't go away. "Try putting them in warm soapy water for a while, then use a soft sponge to rub over them. If that doesn't work, we can try some bi-carb soda in hot water for a while."

In the end I used both methods to finally get them shining again. I found that both had been engraved. One was "Gabrielle 11-9-2003" and the other, "Danielle 12-9-2003".

"That's odd," I told my mother. "They are twins, but one was born the day after the other."

"It can happen," Mum assured me. "If the mother had a

long labour."

On the bottom of each mug was engraved the manufacturer's logo. Reading from top to bottom, the matching script read, "Clayton Silverworks Bassenger" with a little castle glyph. For my own information, I did a rubbing of the engravings and a note of the details in my special notebook. Then, using tissues to hold one, I wondered if such gifts were meant to be used or just admired.

As I looked at the mug, I wondered how they had escaped being stolen, if not by Maude's husband, then by the drifters and human flotsam who had squatted in the house. Had none of them realised they were solid silver? Or had they all assumed, as I had, that they were cheap trinkets. Maude hadn't been rich, and she'd had no one helping her to raise the girls until Delaney married her. So who had given them to her? I noted that thought down, and went to find some tissue paper to wrap them in.

Lucky-pup wanted up, to see what I was doing, but I didn't want her nosing the shiny silver. I held one mug up to show her while my other arm held her away from it. Her little legs were trying to pound the air. I put her down and went back to wrapping. A part of my hand touched the cleaned silver and I did get an image, but not a sad one. I saw a wrapped box, being uncovered and the silver mugs revealed. The wielder discovered the engraving on the bottom and held the mugs to her chest. The emotion I sensed was a mixture of sadness and delight – something like having a secret. Then I saw a hand putting the two mugs into the cabinet where I had found them, sensed rather than heard a whisper of sound like the holder was saying a prayer.

That was enough for one night. I had work to do, though I did a quick internet search for info about the silver works logo. The firm was English, but the name Clayton Bassenger did not show up in relation to it.

While I had the internet open, I checked Facebook. Sometimes, my friends from last year sent messages but Colin never had. I had discovered that he had quickly changed his interest to one of my former classmates. I no longer felt betrayed, there were other nice boys around. This time though, I had a message from "Dusty" – no one I knew. Or did I?

The message read, "FD63, thanks for today. A secret to share?"

Was it Abbie? She's the only one in Victoria that knew my Facebook name. I answered with, "Yes. Fun huh? The big 3 don't know anything." I added a winking emoticon.

If my guess was wrong, the person would wonder at my meaning. However, a reply came back in a little while, just a shades wearing emoticon with a wry smile.

That brought back the flood of images that I'd got when brushing against Abbie at lunch time. Only some had been clear enough to recall now. The strongest was of being in court that morning, enduring a lecture from the judge, and a warning against the repetition. So this time, she wouldn't be sent to a training centre for girls, but did have to do 120 hours of community service. Her father had obviously found a lawyer for her, although I sensed that she didn't like him.

Next in intensity had been how she'd felt after her parents finally returned. Her father seemed to be blaming her for a break in, though it also seemed that Abbie had waited a week before mentioning it. That was damned unfair. Her parents had left her alone for two weeks and no one was lecturing them.

Then there was a tirade of some kind from her father that had really caused Abbie to want to get away. I wished that these images came with sound, but quickly changed my mind. I couldn't imagine my father acting like Mr Carson, or saying anything to make me want to run off.

Abbie had been so upset that she hadn't been thinking straight. I wondered if Adam had received the same sentence.

Abbie had trusted him, but obviously hadn't considered his older brother.

I had gone back to making notes for my essay, when Mum brought in a cup of hot chocolate.

"Dad told me about your friend, Abbie," she commented.

"Oh, yeah. She was an idiot," I said. "She had to go to court, but her friends also got a heavy warning and they are kind of shunning her."

"Why don't you invite her over tomorrow as well?"

"Ah, I kinda think it won't be a good idea. Her dad was furious and has probably grounded her."

Mum nodded, as if that was not unexpected. "You're a good girl, Annie. Though you seem to have landed in interesting times."

"I bet you thought Bellfield was a nice quiet area?"

"I hope you keep using your common sense," she advised.

I had no idea what had brought on this conversation unless it was the fact that I had befriended Martin, who they had heard to have a doubtful reputation. And now Abbie.

Naturally, I promised I would, but added, "I wish Abbie had called me, not Adam. But Gail and Claire were there and she wouldn't want them thinking her friends with me."

"Why ever not?"

Mum was a darling. "Oh, Gail and her group are the rich clique, and since I turned up in second hand stuff they think I'm more of a charity case."

"Does that bother you?"

"No. Gail rules her friends as if she were Cleopatra. Besides, I think Abbie's dad is very image conscious."

"Well, I thought she was a nice girl."

"I hope you agree with me about Martin too." Mum merely smiled. So I added, "I found out that he actually owns the house he lives in. His mother signed it over to him when she split with his dad."

I wasn't going to reveal any more. She didn't need to know as much as I did about his family situation.

"I'll call you when we need picking up," I told my Dad when he dropped Martin and me outside the cinema.

"Don't go wandering around," he told me in return. I wondered if he had read my mind. I pulled a face at him and he just grinned and drove off.

"Maybe you didn't completely impress him," I suggested to Martin who was, for a change, dressed neatly and must have showered after school, before coming to my place.

"Nah! It's probably what he would have done at our age," Martin countered.

I couldn't imagine my dad at fifteen.

"Come on. Let's walk around to the shops."

That was our plan, to look around there and hope to see Maude Delaney. I had a shoulder bag with me that had an old cloth doll with big glass eyes, brown wool hair and a pretty blue and white dress. Mum had helped me wash it, so it looked nearly new.

When I first handled it, I hadn't seen anything, but I had the strangest feeling that I'd had a doll like that when I was small. Mum didn't recall it though. Still, I hoped that Maude would remember it and that would help us get to know her.

As it was Friday night, the shops were still open and lots of people were moving about. Martin had given me a rough idea of what to look for, and I had the picture of Maude from the paper in mind. The doll was in my bag. We both knew this plan was a long shot, and it would be plain luck if she was around when we were.

It took ten minutes to walk to the shops, and we ambled around for a while before Martin suggested we take a break at the coffee shop. I wasn't going to argue. It would be a takeaway drink, since we wanted to get back to the park and have a look around there before going into the cinema. Even Martin agreed that the park, after dark, wasn't the best place to be.

I was hearing a hotted up car engine and was looking around for the source when Martin pulled me into a bus shelter. "Hang back here for a bit, okay?"

"Why?"

"I'll explain later."

I watched Martin stride away, and then slow to a dawdle. The loud engine drew nearer and pulled up alongside Martin. He had obviously known whose car it was, but I did too – from one of Abbie's visions. The driver was Tory Michaelson, the brother of Abbie's friend Adam. The sleaze who had been groping Abbie and trying for more. I didn't want him near me and from the body language he was displaying, I guessed Tory was like Martin's cousins and trying to lord it over him. I would have provided extra ammunition for the guy to use against him.

The conversation was short and Tory got back in his car and roared off. Martin looked my way and beckoned.

"What did he want," I asked.

"He shares my cousins' impression of me, which is that I am desperate enough to want to sell his shit." After a glance at me, I probably had a blank look of non-comprehension on my face, he said, "Drugs. I bet he was the one who got my cousins involved."

"That must be why he can afford that fancy car," I said.

"He reckons he did it up himself," Martin told me. "He has a job with a mechanic."

"Maybe he does, but I don't think doing up a bomb to that standard is cheap."

"I don't dare set the police on him," Martin admitted. His walk changed to be more like it was at school. "I don't need to get a reputation as a police informer."

"Do you think he has any stuff on him?"

"He does. He showed me."

"Well, I had a nasty idea – there's always the Dob in a dealer hotline."

"No, he would assume I had done it anyway."

"Okay, what about an anonymous annoyed female complaining against noise pollution? Do you know his rego number?"

"Yeah. Bond J. Why do you want to bother?"

I told him, "I recognised him from something I saw."

That had Martin's attention. I went on. "I reckon he was trying to do things to Abbie the night she went to Adam's place."

"So that's what he was hinting at. He knew Abbie used to hang out with me. Yeah, do your annoyed female thing. Don't say you know him, they can check the rego. Just say it was a restored Monaro, gold in colour, and where you heard it. You can call the local police. I have a card with their number."

"What about the hoon hotline? If he ever gets to hear where the tip came from he will think 'old, annoyed female'."

Martin chuckled. "Yes, I like that idea."

So I made the call, anonymous – though I bet they had a way of getting my phone number – and gave the information. It might have been coincidence, or luck, that a police car was nearby, but one passed us not five minutes later, as we were almost back at the cinema. I watched it disappear down the street, and hoped it would find Tory's car and search it, and him.

Martin, I realised shortly after, was staring at some point across the road. He had grabbed my arm to start pulling me. We had to wait for pedestrian lights, but once across, Martin sped up, heading towards the park. I followed, until he stopped about twenty metres in, and was looking around in frustration.

"Damn it! I lost him."

"Who?"

"That bloke I mentioned the other day. The one I think Maude was with, or following after."

"Do you know who the bloke is?"

"No. I preferred not to ask."

"Why don't you mention it to the police?"

"Kelly? Yeah, maybe."

"Did you mention seeing him with Maude Delaney before?"

"Do you think it might be her husband?" Martin asked.

"If you read the article with the photo, it said Delaney had just got out of jail."

It was my turn to stand and wait while Martin called the young detective. He soon hung up.

"He's busy. They said he'll ring back."

"I like detective Kelly," I said.

"So do I. He has a more open mind than most of his superiors who tend to think of me as a delinquent."

"You are," I grinned. "You told my father we wouldn't be wandering around."

"We aren't going far from the cinema, and it's not dark yet."

"It will be in half an hour," I estimated. "And that is when the picture is meant to start."

I had told my dad it started at seven, but rang back and said the seven o'clock session was booked out and we would go to the eight o'clock session, and be waiting in or near the cinema. The deception couldn't hurt anyone. As I thought that, a little voice in my head said, *"Did Abbie think that when she rang Adam?"*

Martin's phone ringing distracted me from that thought. I listened to him talking to the detective, saying that he had seen the guy again, recalling the woman who had trotted after him, that he thought might be Maude Delaney. He grinned at me as he told Kelly of my interest, listened a bit, described the man as he was that evening, and hung up.

“Well?”

“Kelly remembered you,” Martin teased, “but he said not to go near the bloke – as if I’d want to – but if I saw him again, or saw the woman, to call back. So, what do you want to do? Go back to the cinema, or keep looking around this end of the park.”

“Keep looking!”

In River Park, we moved off the main paths, and I followed Martin who seemed to know the area quite well. He took me through little private clearings, spaces between rings of old trees and down near the river to picnic tables and bbq pits, and past neat flower beds. Most of the time we were not far off the main paths.

"I have a prickly feeling that something is going on around here," Martin said unexpectedly. "I have seen two blokes that I know are detectives, wandering past."

"No reason why they can't," I told him.

"Well, I don't want them to start hassling me."

"Oh!" I realised that I didn't want it either. "Why don't we go back near that ornamental pond with the fountain and ducklings? They were cute."

"Fine. We have still got a while before it is really dark."

"Probably if Maude is around here, the police will see her," I decided. "Speaking of which, I just recognised one of the local policewomen in plain clothes."

We moved back out of sight and I was trying to do so as quietly as Martin. He stopped when we began hearing voices – or rather, one side of an argument.

"Hang onto that and don't let anyone see it."

Martin was inching closer to the voice, as if trying to hear the speaker.

"And stay here! Out of sight. I will be back to get that thing. If anyone starts showing too much interest in you, do you remember where to go?"

After a pause, "How do you know that you stupid bitch? Well you better keep your mouth shut about that and take that thing where I told you, okay?"

Martin pulled me back behind some trees, and watched as a

man emerged, glanced around, and strode away from us. He followed the man for a bit, and then began texting. Moments later, his phone rang, and from what he went on to say, he was reporting what we had seen and heard. Then, after listening for a bit, he scowled and ended the call.

"That's the guy I saw before," Martin explained. "Kelly was very interested, but he told me again to keep away from him. He's pretty sure it's Mickey Delaney."

"Let's see if it was Maude he was talking to," I urged.

"Wait some."

I saw him looking along the path, and echoed his sigh. The policewoman I had recognised, and her partner, were strolling our way.

"Annie, isn't it?" the woman greeted. "Do your parents know where you are?"

"Yes. We are just killing time here until nearer the time the picture we're going to see starts at the cinema."

She accepted that, and merely added to Martin, "Kemple. Are you behaving yourself?"

"It depends whose point of view you are looking from," Martin told her. "That bloke I just told Kelly about won't think so."

"No, but I understand that you think Maude Delaney is around here."

"We haven't seen her, but that bloke was talking to someone," I explained, pointing back towards the trees.

"Stay here," we were told, before they went off to look.

"If they find her there, they'll just drag her off," Martin predicted.

"Then she will be away from that bloke," I said, but I knew what he meant. Who would understand Maude?

The officers returned and come over. "There's no one there now. Either the person left or the guy was talking on his phone. However, if you see anyone, let us know."

Martin temporised. "We'll have to head off soon, but okay."

As soon as they were gone, Martin dragged me through to where he thought the man had been. He stopped near a bench where the grass was springy and bushes grew close behind.

Very quietly, he said, "Get the doll out."

I did so, and sat it between us, like it was a child. In a whisper, I asked, "Do you think she is still around?"

Martin nodded, but he didn't look around. I had the feeling that he thought she would come to us. I took the doll and bounced it on my lap.

"I hope they catch the bastard," Martin said in a normal voice.

A voice, coming apparently from the bushes behind us, said, "Bad, bad, bad man."

Martin gave the bush a glance. "Yeah, he is."

I said, "Hello Maude, I'm Annie. I brought a friend to see you."

The figure crawled out from under the bush – awkwardly, as if clasping something under her over-sized cardigan. "Ellie's doll. She cried and cried."

"She was at the house. The ones the scouts are fixing up."

"Bad place for family. Good place for scouts."

"My dad is going to help renovate it." I waited for the woman to make sense of my words and reply.

"Yes, good!"

Martin inserted a question. "Did bad man make you hide something?"

"Not yours!"

"Oh, I don't want it," Martin said quickly. "Is it man's?"

"Not his."

"If he stole it, you could give it to the police."

"No trust police."

"Good point," Martin agreed. "Some of them are better than others."

"Too many shadows." That was the first spontaneous comment they'd heard from Maude. "Mickey scared."

Martin and I exchanged glances. He mouthed, "Shadows?"

I glanced skywards. The sun had almost set. Were the shadows from the coming darkness?

Someone came forcing their way through the bushes. Martin stood up, noticing that Maude had left before the man emerged. I scrambled to my feet as the man grabbed the front of Martin's jumper. "You better not be waiting for your old man's cut."

"No way." Martin assured him.

"What you here for anyway, boy?"

I moved closer to Martin and the man leered. "You seen an old homeless bitch?"

"No," I said immediately. "We came in here to be alone."

The man chortled. "You ain't done so well so far."

"You don't have to stay," Martin suggested.

For an answer, the man shoved Martin, who stumbled into me, knocking me over as well. He laughed again, then went off still chuckling and muttering, "Where are you, Bitch? I need that thing."

"Bastard," Martin muttered as he got back to his feet and gave me a hand up.

"Bad, bad, bad indeed," I agreed, looking around. "Did you see where Maude went?"

"No, but the doll is gone. And she left her bag." Martin pounced on something in the underbrush. "That guy has to be her husband."

"Are you going to ring Kelly?" was my suggestion. "Try and tell him she'd got something he wants, but doesn't want him to have it."

"Did you get that by touching her?"

"Just a flash, yep. I reckon the coward's got her to hold onto that thing – whatever it is – so if he was caught, he didn't have it. I think he must have just arranged to hand it over.”

“That might explain all the police around here,” Martin considered. He began texting on his phone.

“I’m glad she hid from that bloke, but I hope we can find her again.”

From somewhere nearby, they heard a phone ring, and soon after, a string of curses.

“You have the wrong bloke, you morons. I’m just trying to find my wife. The bitch is addled in the head, and wandered off. She needs her meds.”

I shook my head. “I wonder if Maude is as addled as people think. Let’s keep looking. She can’t have gone far.”

# Episode 7

# Finding Mad Maude

## Chapter 1

"It's stopped moving," the women who was peering through the night-vision binoculars murmured. "I think he has given it to someone else."

"Keep your eyes on it," the man beside her directed, as he used his own binoculars to scan for his target. "I'll get out there. What are the coordinates?"

"Sector 3. I see three normal heat signatures there now."

The man left, but the woman could hear what he was saying over her headpiece. "Sector 3. Unit 2 move in. Three unknowns. All other units, watch out for Delaney."

As the net closed in on the man who had stolen a prototype power unit, the woman watched the bright orange glow. The unit was emitting heat – a bad sign. Delaney, who was nothing more than a petty thief and drug dealer, must have tried to open it, and played with the interface program.

During the theft of the prototype, which was being transported along with common electrical goods, one man had been bashed and another killed. Delaney would not have expected the armed guard, and must have wondered what the odd device was. Somehow, he had then made contact with the people who were meant to receive it.

Between one heartbeat and the next, the bright glow vanished. "Shit! The glow has gone," the woman exclaimed.

Moments later, in her headpiece she heard, "The two Serbians just took off. Something spooked them. Their contact is ringing someone."

A faint laugh came through the headpiece. "They have Delaney. He should have put his phone on silent. He's a strong brute, but he's no match for the two special operations guys."

"There has to be another one of them somewhere," the woman reminded them all. "We have to find that box. Have the programmer standing by."

Special operative Wanda Davis gave the River Park area another scan before deciding to join the search on foot. She didn't leave the balcony through the house, just climbed over and dropped to the ground. In a suit of mottled dark colours, she was like a wraith, but other dark clad figures were moving around like shadows. Some were on her team, and they had IR-glow tags on their cuffs to identify them.

The others, were the really dangerous men, who would stop at nothing to get their hands back on the hottest piece of stolen merchandise since the Hope Diamond was taken. It was an exciting new discovery – something that would revolutionise the power supply industry. Yet it could probably be used for other things and she feared that it had been terrorists who had executed the original heist.

The woman neared sector three. "Any signs of the box?"

"No. Just a couple of kids. There must be some kind of tracker on that box, since there are a number of shadows lurking."

"Have the perimeter move in. I will keep looking."

Something was drawing Wanda towards the rotunda on the river bank. It was used by wedding photographers by day, and drug dealers by night. Through the binoculars, the woman caught a flash of the bright orange glow. Whoever had it was trying not to be seen, but the fool would have to be very lucky not to be killed by the shadow men. Delaney and his cohorts were probably disposable mules – definitely not in the same league as the original thieves, now trying to get the object back.

Only when she had rushed the crouched figure, grabbing the very warm to touch box, did she realise that it was a woman. A frightened and unsuspecting pawn.

The woman gave a short scream and curled into a small ball.

"Damn it! Dav, sector 5. Some homeless woman had it."

"On my way! Run! You've been spotted."


The scream had carried. David Davis was already racing that way. "Move in now!" he spoke into his radio, "Agent 3 has the object."

The two teenagers he had spotted earlier and unit two arrived first. The girl crouching beside the curled up woman with hands on her ears.

"You kids shouldn't be here. You are in the middle of a police operation."

"Then why aren't you going after the bastard who attacked Maude?" the boy demanded.

"I think she is hurt," the girl added.

"Do you know her?" David asked.

"Her name is Maude Delaney. She's...not the fastest or brightest person. I think her so-called husband was using her to hide something so he could get away."

"Annie, you don't know that. Anyway, that other bastard probably took it from her."

"I will get a medic here to check her over," David promised. Then with obvious disgust, he added, "Another point against Mickey Delaney."

"Shouldn't we get her somewhere else?" the boy asked.

"She'll be fine here for a while. Both of you will stay here too," David directed. Then he spoke softly into his radio. "Sector 5. Three civilians, one down. All bogeys gone."

Even with the gentle pleading of the girl, the woman wouldn't relax from her rigid position. David didn't approach her, he and the two men of unit two kept looking outward, keeping alert for moving shadows.

Shortly, a line of police moved past them. Hand gestures and the tagged cuffs, visible in the parks night lighting, identified the three standing adults as part of the elite squad. The police moved on in silence. Another group would be moving in from the other end of the park, and more would be watching the river frontage and the back walls of the houses abutting the park.

"Hey, what's going on? What's this police operation?" the boy demanded.

David replied, "I'm sure by morning the media will be over it. Do your parents know you are out this late?"

"I told my dad that Martin and I were going to the pictures. I'm to call him when it gets out and he will be picking us up."

"Why don't you call him now?" David suggested.

Martin was in no hurry to urge her to comply. Night had fallen now, but there was enough ambient light for him to judge that the soft spoken American was wearing a flak jacket in addition to the high tech communications gear. He wasn't acting like a policeman, but he might have been the man he'd seen at the police station. He certainly had an aura of confidence that suggested that he'd have no trouble handling a couple of nearly adult children. He was more curious as to why three similarly attired men were guarding them. Did they think that they were part of whatever was going on? The American accent suggested that this was not just a local matter. He wondered too, if his father had been part of it. Not that he cared. He just wanted to know so he could be prepared when the details got out.

He was glad that they had found Maude Delaney. He was impressed by Annie wanting to help her. The older woman was more deserving of help than his father, and certainly needed a champion. He hoped Annie's folks would be decent about her deception. They might have second thoughts about him after this. It would be the third time that she had been involved with the police since she'd met him.

"What about Maude?" Annie demanded. "She doesn't have anyone to care about her."

"I will see the medicos check her over."

"No! No! No hospital."

David glanced down at the crouching woman. So, she was able to hear.

"Look, she's frightened and we just found her. I could take her to my parents place. My Mum is a nurse."

"What is she to both of you?" David asked.

The boy, Martin, retorted belligerently, "It's a long story."

A grin emerged on David's face. "It probably is. The point is, that your friend will need to tell us what her part was in this... ah, don't get all het up...If Delaney is her husband, she might help the police put him away again."

"I don't like the idea of some bull of a policeman asking her questions," Martin insisted.

"OK, no bulls," David agreed as if making a mental note. He was hearing reports via his headpiece, and held a hand up for silence. The watchers saw him go tense, and then relax. "Roger control. I need a medic in sector 5 and a police escort for a witness." He paused then went on, "No, Sir. An ambulance is not required. Just somewhere friendly and quiet. I will organise a car."

"You said..." Martin began.

"Annie. Ring your father. How soon can he get here?"

"Less that ten minutes."

"Okay. Let's head back to the street. I think you all should get away from here before the media descends. Someone in one of the nearby properties must have alerted them."

Annie pressed the fast call button for her home, and explained where they would be waiting, then added, "Um, Dad, we ah...

will have someone else with us....We found Maude. Tell you about it at home."

"Is he going to go off at this?" David asked.

Martin smirked. "Probably if he sees you dressed like that, and armed. Two of you dressed like that in fact."

A new voice spoke. "I am not armed."

David turned and grinned in relief. "Everything safely stowed?"

"Of course! Who do we have here?"

"Annie and Martin and their friend Maude. Can you check her over? We'll have a ride coming."

"The car will only fit three," Martin remarked, eyeing the woman who had helped him the previous week.

"No problem. The police escort will be here soon."


"What's your name?" Annie asked the woman when she realised she was the promised medic.

"It's Wanda. What happened here?"

Annie told her what she knew, finishing with, "And then someone knocked her over and took a box from her."

"Box was warm," Maude finally raised her head.

"Yes, it was. Are you cold, Maude?" Only a small tentative nod indicated an affirmative.

Wanda twisted a backpack to her front and rummaged in it. The small package, when opened, revealed a folded piece of silvery fabric.

"This is a space blanket," Wanda explained, talking to her patient. "Let's get it around you. Are you hurt anywhere?"

"Arm hurts. Fell on it."

"Let me examine it. Tell me if I hurt it more."

Wanda felt over the arm, gently. She felt no reaction from the woman until she reached the upper arm – almost at the shoulder. Then she moved the silver blanket, and the sleeve of the light cardigan the woman had over her dress. She used a small torch to examine the huge bruise there. No fall would have bruised her there.

"How did you get the bruise, Maude?"

The woman didn't answer. "Okay, we can discuss that later. The arm isn't broken, just grazed. I will put stuff on that later. Your friend here, Annie, wants to take you to her place. Are you happy with that?"

"Don't want to go home. Mickey will find me."

"He won't find you at Annie's, and I will see that a nice policeman will keep Mickey away."

"You're nice," Maude said unexpectedly. "You took the box and all the scary shadows went away. Box was warm though."

"Yes. Can you get up now, Maude?"

"I'm strong. Arm don't hurt now."

Annie, on Maude's other side, helped Wanda lift Maude to her feet.

"Was that you who knocked her down?" Annie asked accusingly.

"I wasn't expecting...well, I saw the box and had a chance to snatch it."

"You got it away then?"

"Yup. Safe as if it were in Fort Knox now."

"What was it?"

"Next question," Wanda evaded.

"You won't tell me because I am just a kid!"

"No, because I will be in more trouble than you, if I do."

Annie laughed. "Okay, I get it."

"What's your address, Annie?"

Annie told her and was then asked, "Who are your parents?"

"Henry and Marilyn Jamieson. Mum's a nurse. Dad's a builder and architect. What are you?"

"Well, tonight I was being a hot shot trouble shooter out to pinch a box from the wrong hands. Now, I am the closest paramedic."

"I'd bet that's not all you do," Martin said with a faint grin.

Wanda shot him a grin in return.

Annie didn't need to touch Wanda to agree. "You must be alright. Maude took to you right away."

"I think some peace and quiet was what was needed."

Maude nodded to that.

"Do you need to take any medications, Maude?"

"My bag! I dropped it!"

"Doug has it. I'll have him bring it over," David assured her. "Is that your ride pulling up?"

"Yes. That's Dad."

"Okay. Let's go see if he's going to freak out."


The group approaching the car caused Hank Jamieson to get out. He hadn't missed the way the two rearmost were scanning the area as if guarding his daughter, young Martin, and whoever was helping his daughter with someone else.

"Okay, Annie. What have you got yourself into now?"

"Dad, this is Maude. You know, the lady who used to live in the scout house."

"And?" he queried mildly.

David turned his attention to the girl's father. "Sir, your daughter and her friend have been very helpful. They identified a wanted man and called it in, so that now he is in custody."

The figure between Annie and the other woman tried to dance a jig.

"You have some ID, I suppose."

David moved forward and drew out a lanyard with two laminated cards attached. He proffered the cards to Jamieson whose expression of raised brows betrayed his surprise. He examined the other. "Consultant to the Atlas task force? I haven't heard of that? Is that a local entity?"

"No, multi-national."

"So, what has been going on around here?"

"A very successfully concluded operation," David summarised.

"No doubt the details will be in the papers tomorrow. I have word that the media are besieging the control centre and I think you might prefer that your daughter keeps out of that spotlight."

"Too damn right," Jamieson agreed. "Annie, I hope this isn't going to become a habit."

Wanda spoke softly. "A caring heart shouldn't be discouraged."

"And you are?" Jamieson was beginning to smile.

David answered. "These days she's my mate. When she was your daughter's age, she was the brat from hell."

The man laughed. "Sounds like you are telling me to count my blessings. Are you coming with us?"

"Yes, this should be our ride now. One of the local unmarked police cars."

Very quietly Annie let out a sigh of relief. Her Dad wasn't going to be mad.  She heard Martin whisper, "They're good, those two."

When the two car convoy pulled up at a neat suburban house, Wanda told the police driver, "I would like to go in and talk to Annie's mother before I bring Maude in."

Detective Kelly thought for a moment and merely nodded. He saw the sense in it. Bringing someone in to a stranger's house, who had a nickname of 'mad' needed some preparation. Wanda exited the car quickly and went to talk to the driver of the other car.

Hank Jamieson, who had been wondering how to introduce his unexpected passenger and guests, was quite glad to agree. "Come on in and meet my wife."

The front door opened just as they got there. Marilyn Jamieson was about to speak when she noticed Wanda with her husband. She changed what she was going to say to, "You're not Maude."

"Ah, no," Wanda agreed. "However, I wanted a quick word with you before the others come in, and to apologise for the invasion."

"Do come in."

"I'll just head back to the car," her husband decided.


Wanda followed her hostess through a doorway off the front hall.

"Firstly, I'm Wanda." The official ID laminates were lifted to be shown.

"You are somewhat out of your usual jurisdiction, aren't you?"

"Indeed I am, and responsible for suggesting we bring Maude here. She had the bad luck to be dominated by one of the people that were arrested tonight. You have heard of Maude, it seems."

"Yes, my daughter has developed a concern for her."

Even though the words stayed unsaid, the 'mad' description

seemed to hang in the air.

"And Maude does have need for caring champions," Wanda said. "Please let me assure you that Maude won't be a danger to anyone here or herself. She was released from the Institution where she was committed and has been living in a community house for several years."

"I'd heard some about her," Marilyn admitted. "She once lived in the house which the scouts are doing up. The locals around here say she was always simple, not dangerous, until she took those children."

"Yes, that's what I understood. I suggested the need to talk to Maude away from the police station where they will be processing the people arrested. One of them was her husband, Mick Delaney."

"Shouldn't she have a lawyer, and shouldn't the police be here?"

"Well, Detective Kelly, who I believe you have met, is here and if you have no objection, will stay around overnight, as will I. My husband will only be here for a short while."

"I don't know where you will all sleep. I only have one spare bed."

"Kelly and I can make use of a chair. We will take turns at being awake. As for questions, most of that will wait until tomorrow. I do want to do an assessment of her first. I have had training in emergency medicine and psychology. I believe you are an experienced nurse. I'd appreciate any insights you have as well."

"Of course," Marilyn agreed, as they both heard what seemed to be a crowd entering.

Wanda moved back to Maude as she came in the door, and urged her forward to meet Annie's mother.

"Mum, this is Maude," Annie said, looking to see her mother's reaction.

Wanda added, "Maude, this is Marilyn Jamieson, our

hostess for tonight."

"I've thanks. Not go with Mickey tonight."

Martin Kemple, edging in after Kelly, said, "He's where he belongs."

David, Wanda's husband, came in last and muttered, "Let's hope he stays there."


Just at that moment, loud yipping began from further in the house.

"Doggy? Like Doggy," Maude announced.

"I'll introduce you to Lucky-pup later," Annie promised.

At the same time, Marilyn spotted Martin. "Hello, did you get to the pictures after all? Oh, and who else do we have here?"

Wanda introduced David, adding, "He needs to report back to the police higher ups."

"Well, come in and sit down. I've the kettle on for hot chocolate. Hank, shut the door, will you? Annie, go talk to that dog of yours. Don't let her out unless you can hold onto her."

"I'll go with you." Martin moved off after Annie. "I should be able to hold that wriggling dervish."


With Maude keeping close to Wanda, still hugging the doll Annie had returned to her, and sitting herself on the front edge of the couch, the invasion settled down. Kelly, David and Hank chose to stay standing, observing rather than participating, leaving Wanda in control.

"Maude, would you like a drink of hot chocolate?"

"Not hot."

"Cold?"

"Not cold."

"Warm?"

Maude nodded. Wanda said, "I'll have the same please." The others gave their preferences.

The noisy yapping ceased and Maude whispered, "Who strangers?"

In a low voice, Wanda explained, "The nice policeman Kelly, Mr Jamieson, our other host, and my mate, David."

Once the mugs of hot drinks had been distributed, and a plate of biscuits put on the table, Annie and Martin reappeared with the small dog, now quiet, but when she smelt other people began wriggling again.

"Okay you silly mutt, we will go and meet everyone, but I am not letting you go!" Martin muttered.

A brief pat or scratch from the others satisfied the dog, who was more reserved when Martin passed her to Annie, who let her sit on the lap of a delighted Maude.

"Soft," she whispered, as she put aside the rag doll and continued to pat the pup.

Wanda knew David needed to go off, but at the same time, she did not want to overwhelm Maude. Instead, she urged Maude to drink and have a biscuit while Annie and her mother went off to get the spare bed ready. The little dog showed no sign of wanting to move and Maude was slowly relaxing.

"Mickey certainly put you in a bad spot tonight," Wanda commented.

"Put himself. Shouldn't take thing. Wasn't his."

"True," Wanda agreed. "We will need to talk about that tomorrow. Will you remember?"

"I do. Good memory."

"Always?" Wanda prompted.

Maude didn't answer that right away. Wanda gave her time to think.

"No. Not around Mickey. Then only sometimes."

"Why might that be?" Wanda asked.

"Not like Mickey. Got me meds. Not same as have."

Detective Kelly came closer and crouched in front of Maude, deliberately coming down to her level.

"Do you have your meds here?"

David spoke from near the door. "I'm minding them."

"Who is your usual doctor?" Kelly asked. "I can check with him before you take any more."

Maude chuckled. "Not been taking them sometimes. Then remember better."

"Your doctor?" Kelly prompted.

"Charlie Burrows. Name like rabbit hole."

"Do you know his phone number?"

"No. Matron calls him."

"That's okay. I can contact her."

Wanda asked, "Would Matron know who to call to have someone with you tomorrow for questions?"

"Trusty guy."

"You have trustees?" Wanda guessed aloud. "Do you know their number?"

This time Maude answered with a string of numbers and phrases as if she were singing a jingle. Wanda memorised what she said.

"I'll organise that," Kelly offered. "The Hartley Trustees pay for her accommodation and care. I know the firm they belong to."

"Castletown. Trustee is King."

"Excellent. We will have Mr King or a representative available tomorrow," Wanda said quickly.

Annie and her mother returned from making the spare bed. "I'm going to need to get some sleep. I'm on early shift," Marilyn Jamieson announced. "And it is past Annie's bedtime."

"I'll drop Martin back home," Hank Jamieson offered.

"No need, Sir," David countered. "Our driver has to take me back. We can drop Martin on our way."

"I could walk," Martin announced. "But, I won't say no to a lift. Ah, Mr Jamieson, when will you be helping out with the scout house next?"

"Sunday. Baxter is trying to organise to remove all the rubbish. Are you planning to help?"

"I'd be interested."

Hank winked, but said neutrally, "I am sure Baxter won't say no."

Wanda took out the empty cup to wash while Annie helped her mother settle Maude. Kelly followed her.

"Well, what do you make of her?"

"Maude? I was expecting simple, childlike, and she is. No one has expected her to be like an adult since she came out."

"But?" Kelly prompted.

"Well, you will need to take this on faith, and I urge you to suggest she has an updated psychological examination, but I can feel that there is a great deal more going on in Maude's mind than she is able to express."

"I thought telepathy was a myth," Kelly murmured.

Wanda looked sharply at him.

"It's what my Nan always said," Kelly said quickly, as he shrugged. "But my grandpa had other ideas."

"Well, yes it's a myth...mostly," Wanda told him.

Kelly decided to change the topic. "I will have her medicine checked. What do you expect us to find?"

"That they aren't her usual meds. Likely the evening ones

are sleeping pills, and the day ones...something psychoactive, to addle the mind. David described them to me, and what the label says on the bottle doesn't match. However, I am not an expert and the way medicines look here maybe different to at home. In any case, the result will be interesting."

"She remembers better when she doesn't take them," Kelly recalled Maude's comment.

Wanda dared to make a comment of her own. "And maybe when she is taking them, her mind is less clear, and she can't reason. Tonight she certainly knew Mickey had stolen something."

She let Kelly consider that for a bit before suggesting, "Sunday, if Maude is not needed for questions, I would like to take her back to that house where she used to live. Annie too, I think."

"Do you expect to find anything?" Kelly sounded like his suspicious police persona.

"I have no idea."

"Why suggest it? It might upset her."

"Have you found stuff there? Off the record and on the promise of silence?"

Kelly decided to trust her, and recapped all he knew. He watched as Wanda took it in and considered the ramifications. He knew that she, and her husband, were US State Department investigators, and his grandfather thought highly of them, and had been the one to request their help. Now he realised that there was more about them than what was obvious. She did not explain her thoughts however.

"I just wondered if Delaney was using some odd drugs on her now, and we have no proof yet, was he doing the same years back. I doubt if I would be able to have access to Maude's old psych examinations from before her committal, but..."

He caught the innuendo. "Her mind is clearer when Mickey isn't around." He stopped short of saying what had just occurred to him, that Delaney had contrived Maude's conviction. He couldn't think of reason why he would.

Wanda, who could indeed sense thoughts, was satisfied that he would be open to that idea. "So, what say I have first watch?"

Hank Jamieson and Kelly moved one of the lounge chairs into the spare bedroom. Wanda settled there after asking Maude if she minded the company. When the men had left, Maude spoke softly.

"Can't sleep."

"So much has happened today, it isn't surprising," Wanda reassured her. She noted that the rag doll was tucked half under the pillow.

"You sleep in chair?"

"Later, yes. I have done enough of it."

"You have little ones?"

"Yes, a boy who is four and a girl who is two."

"What called?"

"Davy, after my husband, and Katy after my mother."

"Davy, Katy. Nice. Like Gabbie and Ellie. Where they?"

"My kids? Oh, staying with my sister, who usually takes them to visit their uncles, aunts and Grandpa."

"My girls...don't know where. Mickey said, took away for look after."

"Did he? Why did he do that?"

"I hit head. Went to hospital."

"How did you hit your head that hard?"

"Mickey said I did."

Wanda allowed herself to sense the thoughts in Maude's mind. Memories. Mickey was a bastard, often hitting her. "Why ever did you marry him?" She waited for Maude to answer.

"Nice he was. Good in bed. Liked that. Changed later."

"Happens too often."

"Mama wanted me marry. Not old maid. Better as not single mum."

"Did Mickey like your girls?"

"No time for them. Always working."

"How long did you live together?" Wanda was wondering why Mickey did marry her, and if it was a proper ceremony.

"Married in June. Got took away in October."

"Well, I think you should divorce him. Is he still good to you in bed?"

"Still good," Maude whispered. "But bad, bad, bad man. Know now."

"You deserve better, Maude."

"Who want me now?"

"How do you get on at the place where you were staying before Mickey came back?"

"Friends there. Mind kept busy. Good place."

"So why ever did you go back with Mickey?"

"We married. Said we should."

"Do you still feel that way?"

"No, no, no. Don't know why I did. Mickey trouble."

"I hope he goes away for a very long time," Wanda said. "But you should tell your trustee guy that you don't want to stay married to him. You're better off with just friends."

"You friend. Good friend. I like you. Like little Annie too."

"I'll be your friend, and not just to help get Mickey put away. Except, my home is far away in America."

"Can write letters," Maude suggested. "I read good."

"Do you use computers?" Wanda wondered aloud.

"Rubbish in, rubbish out." Maude chuckled. "Tried though."

"But you write?"

"Get friend to write. What on paper, what in head that way."

"I see," Wanda mused. "How are you with numbers?"

"I count okay."

"Is that all?"

"Why ask?"

"I want to try an experiment. Can you do sums on paper?"

"Answer never right."

"What about in your head?"

"Think right there."

"Okay. Do this just in your head. I will ask you to add two numbers, and just think of the answer."

"How you know it?"

"My secret, okay. I will tell you the answer you worked out. You say if I am right."

Wanda did this for a while, making the sums gradually harder and more complex. When Maude finally fell asleep, she had proof that the older woman's mind was far from simple.

Wanda slept for four hours before waking again at six when the Jamiesons began stirring and a refreshed puppy began racing around to check the strangers. Not unexpectedly, Annie followed to collect her dog.

"I'm sorry. I have to put her in the laundry for now," she told the two guests. "Mum has to go to work, but I will make you breakfast when you want it. And I have some things for Maude."

"For me?" Maude's eyes widened.

"Things I found at the house that I thought you might want," she explained.

"You nice girl," Maude said as thanks.

"I'll just go and speak to your mother before she goes," Wanda murmured. "I would like to thank her."


In fact, Wanda wanted to get Marilyn Jamieson's opinion of Maude.

"Maude is childlike and you were right. I don't think she would deliberately hurt anyone. However, I am neither a psychiatrist nor a psychologist," was the comment.

"What would you say if I suggested that there is a lot more going on in her head than she can express? That her mind isn't simple?"

"It's possible, I would think. I don't know how you could show it."

"That is still the problem. Never mind though. Do you think she was born that way?"

"I can't say. Though you might find out. Some of the people hereabouts know the family. Probably her trustees would know."

"I mean to ask them, but I wanted your thoughts first."

"The trouble may have happened during birth, or an accident while she was an infant," Marilyn finally suggested. "That's just my opinion. You would need to ask an expert."

"It will do as a working hypothesis for my own reasons."

Maude was delighted to be able to choose her breakfast rather than have it just put in front of her. She seemed like a child having a party. The illusion increased when Annie produced the box of things she had saved from the house clean up.

She took out the cleaned picture frames first and passed them over. Maude's eyes widened, then glistened with incipient tears. "Little Gabbie, little Ellie. My girls." Maude had pointed to each girl as she named them.

"They look happy," Annie said. "Clean and healthy."

"I be good mum. Loved them."

"There were two slides with hair in them," Annie said. "But I think the police kept them." She glanced at Kelly for confirmation.

"They will be returned when we finish with them," he said.

"Why you need?" Maude asked, looking at them.

Kelly shifted his position in the lounge chair. "To determine if some organic matter was human or animal."

"You don't need DNA for that," Annie blurted.

Wanda knew of the bones they had found, and so did Annie, but she realised that Maude had also made the connection and was getting upset. She touched Maude's hand and suggested, "That's too scientific for this time of the day. What else is in that box?"

As she hoped, Maude was diverted. Annie lifted two tissue wrapped objects, and watched as Maude carefully unwrapped them.

"Oh! Clay give. This is Ellie's. This is Gabbie's."

"Mum said they were solid silver. Valuable," Annie said. "She told me how to clean them. Did you hide them from Mickey?"

Maude chuckled. "Not his. Belong to girls."

"I'm surprised no one found them," Annie remarked.

"I say words. I say hide from bad man."

Annie didn't know what to say to that, so she looked in the box again. "I was going to clean up more of the things. The rest of the stuff is very dusty." She rose and went to moisten a sponge at the kitchen sink and grab a tea towel.

"I think these are baby records from the health nurse," Annie said after wiping the sponge over a plastic folder.

"Say I did good for girls," Maude said proudly, before opening one and glancing through the pages. Wanda took it from her and scanned the pages. Maude was right.

Next, Annie pulled out two pairs of dusty, once white, baby shoes. She quickly wiped them all over.

Noticing how quickly Annie dropped each one, Wanda studied the teenager and saw she had paled. Maude, reached out and arranged the shoes in their correct pairs after glancing at the soles.

"When are we going to be needed by the task force, Kelly?' Wanda asked.

"Nine o'clock or when we get there."

Wanda nodded. Her question was aimed at distracting Annie, this time.

"The rest of the stuff is just odds and ends." She pushed the box to Maude, who rummaged around and pulled out a brown box that proved to contain letters. These she clasped to her chest.

The body language alone told Wanda that they were indeed special, but she didn't probe Maude's mind or ask about them.

"Any chance of some coffee?" Kelly asked hopefully, as Hank Jamieson returned from an errand to the shops.

"I'll do it," Annie volunteered.

Hank put several papers on the table. "So the fuss was about some hi-tech prototype gadget. So where did my daughter fit into all this?"

"Just a coincidence being nearby," Wanda assured him.

Maude said, unexpectedly, "Mickey had it. Made me have it. She took it!" Her finger pointed at Wanda who just grinned.

"Get that look off your face, Kelly. I had it last. I still have to work out how a low-life like Mickey knew about it."

"We have some theories," Kelly assured her. He lifted the top paper, the Herald Sun, to look for the article which he found on page three. Wanda reached for The Age. She watched Kelly frown as he read. Then he looked at the one in The Age. In it was the revelation that the leader of the group of thieves had escaped capture. Though Wanda had hoped otherwise, she wasn't surprised. The man belonged to an international crime ring she called The Family.

"Mickey must have been cannon fodder," she said, likening the local criminal to the throw away soldiers in some video games.

"Thinks he knows all, Mickey does."

Wanda was inclined to agree, but if Mickey had been working for The Family, it was so they didn't risk one of their own. "I bet you could tell us all sorts of things about Mickey," she suggested to Maude.

She chuckled. "I know things he don't know I know."

"Maybe you can share those things with Detective Kelly's colleagues later. I will be there to help."

"So you won't let them bully her," Annie pleaded, looking at Wanda who shook her head.

Wanda was about to add something else when her phone vibrated in her pocket. "Ah, excuse me," she said, moving off to take the call in private.


The caller was, as she had guessed, David, who after exchanging personal greetings told her, "I located the head of Maude's trustees. He is sending a Robert Tyrell. Maude knows him even though he is not the regular one to handle her account. He sounds like a really cluey guy and has known the Hartley family from way back. He will have one of their legal team come to the station.”

“I want to talk to him,” Wanda told her mate. “Can you arrange that?”

“Done. Anything else?”

“You heard that a guy got away?”

“Yes, and he is likely already out of the country. A problem?”

“No, unless they want us to go after him right away.”

“What is going through that sneaky mind of yours?”

“A nice little mystery. Which, you will tell me is none of my business, but I think I need to help a couple of people.”

“Maude?” David guessed. “Who else?”

“I will tell you later. But it might interest you to know that Detective Kelly is open to the idea of my little foibles.”

Wanda saw Annie hanging back, waiting for her to finish talking, and cut off David's reminder that her special extra senses were classified. "I will see you at the police station. Will it be the local one or the city headquarters?"

"In Melbourne. The local one is besieged by media. I will be coming to pick you up."

Wanda returned the phone to her pocket, and smiled at Annie and headed her way.

"Maude said you could read her head. Can you?"

Cautiously, Wanda nodded, wondering what was on the girl's mind.

"Do you sort of get images off things?" Annie blurted.

Wanda made a guess. "Like you can?"

It was Annie's turn to nod cautiously, maybe expecting to be laughed at.

"No, not quite. I often just 'know' things that I shouldn't. It freaks some people."

"Yeah." Annie's laugh was self-conscious. "But what if it tells you things that might be important for someone else to know?"

"Ah, that can be tough. Would you care to share your concerns with me?"

Annie seemed to wriggle on the spot.

"You don't have to," Wanda hurried to assure her. "But just answer this. Are the things you refer to just about Maude? Or does it relate in any way to the events of last night? That is my current priority."

"Mostly just Maude, but it probably isn't vital. Though Martin and I heard someone talking to her. The guy had a word with Martin too."

"Hmm. Let me have a word with Kelly. I might get you to come with us, Martin too. So you can mention that. Do you think your dad will object?"

"Maybe not if you ask him."

"Okay then. And sometime less hectic, you and I should talk. Maybe Sunday, at the scout house."

"I'd like that," Annie admitted. She looked happier and managed a smile.


Police headquarters in the city was almost overwhelming to most of the group waiting by the lifts on the ground floor. While waiting, most were watching the activity around them. When the lift pinged its arrival, they did not expect the man who strode out of the lift, almost walking into Martin and shoving past Annie, as he hurried out of the building.

"What the heck," Martin murmured.

"Was that Abbie's father?" Annie asked him.

"Sure looked like him. Wonder why he was here. Certainly wanted out in a hurry."

"I hope it is nothing to do with Abbie."

Wanda moved around to Annie and asked quietly, "Are you all right?" Annie nodded, saying nothing, just staring after the figure.

Maude tugged on Wanda's sleeve. "Know him, I think."

Martin heard and said quietly, "His name is Jeremy Carson."

Maude shook her head. "Not that name."


Two men entered the front door. David walked forward to meet them and Maude followed.

"Mr Tyrell," David greeted. One of the men nodded as David introduced himself and added, "Thanks for coming."

"This is Joe Elliot, one of our legal team," Tyrell introduced in turn. "We are hoping to have a chance to talk with Maude before she has to face questions."

"I will request it," David promised.

While Tyrell greeted Maude, Elliot moved close to David.

"You look well, my dear girl. Whatever have you got into now?"

"Help fix Mickey."

Tyrell's face hardened. "So, that's where you disappeared to. We've been worried."

"Want to un-marry him," Maude announced.

"Indeed, my girl. We'll discuss that later."

"Good. You see man who left?" Maude asked.

Wanda saw Tyrell's frown of confusion and added, "The one who stormed out as if the posse was after him – as you came in."

"Yes, I did. Thought I knew him. Can't place him though."

"Two of Maude's friends think his name is Carson," Wanda suggested.

"Carson? No, I don't recall anyone of that name."

"Still think know him," Maude continued. "Saw him. With you. Nice man. Long ago."

"I will try to recall," Tyrell promised.

"Me too," Maude agreed. "Think name. Know him."

Wanda knew all three of the men who met them in the upstairs office. One was the retired Chief Inspector who had requested her and David from the Atlas Task force. The others were local officers also attached to the task force.

The latter two would have preferred to lead the questioning of Mickey Delaney's wife, but had demurred after being briefed by David, who gave them Wanda's evaluation of Maude. Naturally, they had all that was officially known about her, and were sceptical on several levels. One, whether she was mentally sound, and two, if she could accurately answer questions.

Initially, at least, they were willing to let Wanda ask the questions, and passed to her a list of subjects to quiz Maude on. Joe Elliot, who'd had his private chat with Maude, was happy with the arrangements.

Martin and Annie were taken to a side room, where they

would wait with Kelly. David, kept out of the way in the main room, observing proceedings and making his own notes to add to the recording of the interview.

Wanda allowed one of the local officers to provide the required formalities at the start, and then took over smoothly. She began by getting Maude to answer simple questions that told of her recent involvement with her husband. Just from her replies, the listeners were soon sure that Delaney was using her to minimize his own danger. It was also apparent that Delaney did indeed consider her stupid, by the way he had programmed her to carry out the movements needed on the previous day. His reaction to her mentioning his stash places caused the officers to suddenly sit up straighter.

Maude had candidly explained that 'Mickey kept shit there'. That was in reference to the rotunda in the park.

"What about the bike house?" Wanda asked. That had been where Maude should have taken the stolen prototype.

The one question that convinced the listeners that Maude, despite her communication difficulties, was not addled was her answer to, "Why didn't you take it there?"

She had said, "Not his."

At that point, one of the two active officers asked, "How did you know that?"

"Mickey think stupid is deaf."

Wanda, aware that Maude had so much she wanted to express, made a suggestion to give her time to sort it out.

"I'd like to come back to that, but at this point, I think it would be useful to hear what the two young witnesses overheard. Can we bring Martin and Annie in please?"

The two teenagers could only confirm part of Maude's statement, mainly the conversation with Mickey. However, when Martin mentioned Delaney had challenged him about 'his father's cut', the two officers were instantly focused on him.

One asked, "And your father is...?"

"Kevin Kemple."

That one looked to Kelly. "Can we have him brought in later?"

"Easy, Sir. He's being held at the City watch house on a number of assault charges."

"Excellent. Delaney isn't talking, maybe Kemple knows something."

Martin felt his face lose colour. Had his father been mixed up in this? He looked at Wanda, recalling that she had been watching 'known associates' of various people. Had he taken part in the robbery where a guard had died? Had the people using the garage at his house had that object there?

"Kelly, why don't you take Martin and Annie down to get a drink while their recorded answers are transcribed into a statement?" Wanda suggested.

The Story
Continues in

**Touching Other Lives
Volume 2**

Episode 8: More Clues to the Past

Episode 9: More Police Attention

Episode 10: Daddy's Girl

Episode 11: The Tip of the Iceberg

Episode 12: Events Heat Up

Episode 13: Clues Come Together

Episode 14: Carson Under Pressure

Also by Margaret Gregory
<u>TYMOREAN TRUST SERIES:</u> (Fantasy)
Book 1 - Power Rising
Book 2 - Great Ones
Book 3 - The Return to Earth
Book 4 – Earth Mission
Book 5 – Alien Contact
Book 6 - Invasion
<u>ATAPI SORCERESS SERIES:</u> (Fantasy)
Prequel – Korvu: The Beginning
Book 1- The Wild One
Book 2 – Atapi Sorceress
<u>THE THIRD GENERATION SERIES:</u>(Fantasy)
Book 1 - Wanda: From Bad to Worse
Book 2 - Wanda: Choosing Crime
Wanda – Early Days (anthology) Book 1 and 2
Book 3 – Wanda: Risking Life to Live
Book 4 – Erin: The Forcing of Wisdom
Book 5 – Wanda: A New Life Part 1 – Hidden Secrets
Book 6 – Wanda: A New Life Part 2 – First Mission
Book 7 – Wanda: Full Circle
The Serpent's Shadow
Royal Favour
Foreign Agent - Thief
Prisoner - Spy

<u>HOLDER OF SECRETS SERIES:</u>
**Unregarded**
**Unsuspected**
**Unrepentant**

<u>STAND ALONE</u>
The Magpie's Daughter
The Chance to be Me